OUT OF THE SHADOW WORLD

COLLEEN CHAO

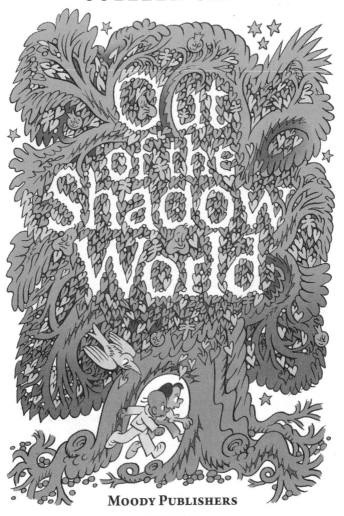

Out of the Shadow World

MOODY PUBLISHERS

CHICAGO

Edited by Amanda Cleary Eastep
Cover and interior illustrations: Benjamin Schipper
Cover and interior design: Erik M. Peterson
Photo credit: Eddie Chao

Library of Congress Cataloging-in-Publication Data

Names: Chao, Colleen, author.
Title: Out of the shadow world / Colleen Chao.
Description: Chicago : Moody Publishers, [2023] | Audience: Ages 10. |
  Audience: Grades 4-6. | Summary: Ten-year-old Pax and his best friend
  Jayni enter a magical realm of bewitching creatures in search of a
  mysterious man who might be able to heal Pax's cancer.
Identifiers: LCCN 2022052098 (print) | LCCN 2022052099 (ebook) | ISBN
  9780802430922 (paperback) | ISBN 9780802473363 (ebook)
Subjects: CYAC: Best friends--Fiction. | Friendship--Fiction. |
  Cancer--Fiction. | Healing--Fiction. | Fantasy. | BISAC: JUVENILE
  FICTION / Religious / Christian / Action & Adventure | JUVENILE FICTION
  / Action & Adventure / General | LCGFT: Fantasy fiction. | Novels.
Classification: LCC PZ7.1.C48245 Ou 2023 (print) | LCC PZ7.1.C48245
  (ebook) | DDC [Fic]--dc23
LC record available at https://lccn.loc.gov/2022052098
LC ebook record available at https://lccn.loc.gov/2022052099

Printed by: Bethany Press in Bloomington, MN, February 2023

Originally delivered by fleets of horse-drawn wagons, the affordable paperbacks from D. L. Moody's publishing house resourced the church and served everyday people. Now, after more than 125 years of publishing and ministry, Moody Publishers' mission remains the same—even if our delivery systems have changed a bit. For more information on other books (and resources) created from a biblical perspective, go to www.moodypublishers.com or write to:

Moody Publishers
820 N. LaSalle Boulevard
Chicago, IL 60610

1 3 5 7 9 10 8 6 4 2

Printed in the United States of America

To Jeremy—
who is learning to live in the shadows
with joyful courage.

CONTENTS

PRONUNCIATION GUIDE

Jayni	JAY-nee
Mersades	mer-SAY-deez
Darya	DAR-ee-uh
Hobblechaun	hobble-kawn
Declan	DECK-len
Fennec	FEN-ek
Marion	MARE-ee-uhn
August	AW-guhst
Ru	roo
Cada	KAY-duh
Chevrotain	SHEV-ruh-tayn

The Climbing Tree

Pax Jackson was a ten-year-old boy who didn't know if he'd make it to his eleventh birthday.

He had gray eyes, a bald head where thick curls used to grow, and a little more of his dad's dark skin than his mom's fair complexion. He also had a nagging cough that rattled his bony body and kept him up at night. Instead of shoving his homework into his backpack and rushing to catch the bus home from school that afternoon, he sat on the back deck of his family's log cabin, dangling his feet over the edge and watching a fat lizard do push-ups in the warm sun. With the sound of his own wheezing loud in his ears, he didn't notice the squeak of the school bus brakes on the street out front.

Jayni Suko was a petite ten-year-old girl with almond

eyes and paper-straight black hair. Stepping off the school bus, she bent forward under the weight of a bulging backpack as she made a detour toward the house next door. She bounded up the driveway of Pax's home and hurried around to the backyard.

"Pax!" Jayni ran up the steps of the deck, dropped her backpack, and sat down beside her friend. She studied Pax's face. "We missed you at school. This a bad day?"

"Yeah." A smile peeked out through the dark circles around his eyes. "What'd I miss?"

"Not much. Miss Halpin gave me your homework but said if you weren't feeling up to it, don't worry. She'll help you catch up later."

Jayni pulled two tattered textbooks out of her backpack and a few wrinkled worksheets and plopped them between her and Pax.

Pax only glanced at his homework, then turned away.

Jayni followed his gaze out over a sloping hill peppered with pine trees.

Jayni was the youngest daughter of the Suko family who'd moved next door to the Jacksons almost twelve years ago. The Sukos and Jacksons had become fast friends, and when Pax and Jayni were born two years later, the neighborhood had grown a little louder and a lot more fun.

Jayni looked over at Pax. "You okay?"

"Yeah, I guess." Pax's voice softened. "I'm glad you're here." The friends sat in silence. The lizard darted away and disappeared under the deck. Pax took a deep, rattly breath.

"Do you think you could make it down to the Climbing Tree?" Jayni asked. "I can help you."

"'Course I can, Spitfire. And I don't need any help."

Spitfire was Pax's nickname for Jayni. He'd read it once in a book about dragons and knights, and it seemed to fit his friend who was as fiery and fearless as a dragon.

Jayni laughed as she hopped up. "I just have to be home by dinner, so we've got two hours. Let's go!"

Jayni reached down for Pax's hand, but he pushed it away, eager to prove he was stronger than he looked.

The two friends descended the deck steps and scampered down a small bank covered in crunchy pine needles. Their footfalls stirred the scent of a thousand Christmas trees into the warm spring air. Pax paused to catch his breath along the way. Ten steps forward, a right at the boulder, a hop across the stream—and there stood the Climbing Tree, like a giant with an oversized head of shaggy hair.

They'd discovered the enormous oak when they were just six years old, and they'd been returning ever since—to dream up stories, build forts, and talk about important kid stuff, like the proper ratio of ketchup to French fry. Sometimes on the weekends or holidays, they'd pack snacks and books and blankets, and read under the expansive branches till the sun got sleepy.

This is also where they'd had their biggest fight, the summer they were seven. And where they'd run to take refuge two years ago—on the day Pax got his diagnosis.

Jayni beat Pax to the tree and lifted a thick, drooping branch high so he could pass underneath. But Pax grabbed the branch himself and waited for Jayni to enter first. She shot him a withering look but marched inside anyway. When Pax let go of the branch, it swished and thudded against the ground. Now safely beneath the canopy of branches, the children headed straight to their favorite spots. Pax chose a low broad limb and slung his body over it like a sloth, arms and legs dangling free.

Jayni scrambled up three limbs above him, leaned back against the trunk, and in a British accent declared, "Behold the Queen of the Climbing Tree! You there, young man, who are *you*? How dare you enter my royal court without permission!"

Pax rolled his eyes, and a smug smile played around his mouth. "Your Royal Fakeness, I am *King* of the Climbing

Tree. You have been found out. Guards, seize her!" He paused to cough before commanding, "Off with her head!"

Jayni's eyes flashed, and she was about to fire back at Pax when she heard a loud rustling sound above her.

"What's that?" she asked, craning her neck to look up into the dark maze of branches.

"Sounded like a bir—" but before Pax could put the *d* on "bird," they heard a peculiar voice say, "Dad-gum it! This tree gets harder to find every time!"

The complaint was punctuated by a wild flapping and the sound of a bell, like the fire alarm at school.

Pax forced himself up into a sitting position, and he and Jayni stretched and strained to see who was at the top of their tree.

The vexed voice spoke again. "Oh, rot and rubbish! These wattles will be the end of me!"

More flapping disturbed the leaves overhead, another shrill bell sounded, and a few brown feathers floated downward. A disheveled bird popped down through the upper branches and began to hop toward them, circling the trunk branch by branch, as if descending a winding staircase.

Pax and Jayni froze. Had this bird just been . . . *talking*? He was an odd-looking thing: his bottom half was rooster-brown, his top half snow white, and every single feather was frizzy and out of place, as if he'd just been struck by lightning. His black eyes bulged and rarely blinked. But his most striking feature was what dangled from the end of his black beak: three, long, rubbery strands that whirled and whipped with his every movement. A leafy twig had become tangled up in one of them, and the bird kept scratching at it with his claws and shaking his head violently, trying to free the thing.

Down and down he came, muttering all the way, feathers flying. He ran right over Jayni, who sat still as a statue, and right past Pax, then spread his wings and fluttered to the ground.

"Now where is that blasted thing?" He bent low, cocked his right eye to the ground, muttered again, shuffled through some leaves, clawed at the tangled twig, then pecked at the ground. "Agh! Well, I am up a creek without my cattle!"

Pax's and Jayni's shocked looks changed to amusement. Pax raised an eyebrow and silently mouthed at Jayni, *without a paddle?*

Jayni nodded, then bit her lip to keep from laughing.

Both children were considering whether to go on in silence or to speak up and reveal themselves when the

bird latched onto a piece of bark with his beak and tugged at it violently. The Climbing Tree quivered and quaked, and—as if a talking bird hadn't been shocking enough— the trunk miraculously swiveled open, revealing a gaping black hole no bigger than the bird.

"Oh!" gasped Jayni and Pax at the same time.

Startled, the frizzy and frazzled bird jerked his head up, sending the tangled twig into a tailspin. On spying the children, his beak opened wide and let loose that awful bell sound. "What! Oh, rot and rubbish. Just my luck. I suppose you both were there the whole time? Saw everything?"

Pax and Jayni couldn't find their words yet, but they slowly nodded.

"Well, I'll be a monkey's brother. Why do these things always happen to me? Collywobbles! You'll both have to come with me, I'm afraid. I can't leave you here now that you've seen the doorway." He stuck out a wing to wave them inside.

Jayni summoned her power of speech and stammered, "But . . . this is *our* tree. We've come here for years, and . . . it's never done *that* before."

Pax, who was terrified of tight, dark spaces, quickly added, "I'm *not* going in there."

Am I seriously arguing with a talking bird? Pax wondered.

Maybe he had fallen asleep on the tree limb, and this was just a strange dream. He'd soon wake up and tell Jayni all about it, and they would laugh together.

The bird cleared his throat and ruffled his feathers. "I'm sorry, but you absolutely must come with me now. What a mess! We'll have to see Declan. He'll know what to do."

"You can't force us to go anywhere!" declared Jayni.

The whole weird encounter was leaving Pax suddenly drained, so he was relieved that Jayni had spoken up.

The bird let out a huff and narrowed his bulging eyes. "Young lady, it's time you faced the musical. The reality is, this is a top-secret tree whose roots lead to great wonders and mysterious places and a healing man, and I can't just have you two—"

"A *healing* man?" interrupted Pax, perking up.

"Why, yes, of course. Ah, gimcrack! I suppose you haven't heard of him *out here.*"

The bird scratched at the tangled twig still dangling from the rubbery beak rope, and he blew his bell again. "Agh! These snag-nabbit wattles!"

Pax was deep in thought about the healing man as Jayni climbed down from her limb, enchanted by the magical creature. "Where are you from? How did you get here?"

But the bird was swinging his head back and forth due

to the twig, so Jayni bent forward and reached toward his beak. "May I?" she asked.

He blinked in surprise, and then said, "Well, um, I suppose so. You look as harmless as a glove."

Jayni giggled. "I think you mean a *dove*."

She carefully unwrapped the twig from the wattle, which she didn't at all like touching—it felt like wormy rubber bands.

"Ahhh. Such sweet relief! Well, thank you, thank you kindly," crooned the bird. With one claw he stroked all three wattles, then fluffed his feathers and sighed.

"Where are you from?" Jayni repeated.

"Mademoiselle, I am a three-wattled bellbird from— ehhh, I'm not sure if I'm allowed to tell you where. But it's not far from here. Not far at all."

Jayni wondered why he couldn't tell her where he was from, but before she could open her mouth to ask any more questions, the bird was prattling on again.

"Ah, look at me forgetting my manners. Mother would be so disappointed. My name is Wilmer. How do you do?" The bird attempted a tottering bow.

Jayni smiled. "How do you do, Wilmer? My name is Jayni, and this," she said, pointing up into the tree, "is my friend Pax."

While Jayni and Wilmer had been chatting, Pax began to feel something he hadn't felt in a very long time. That tiny spark of hope that had been snuffed out by long months of illness suddenly blazed into a forest fire. Somewhere out there was a healing man, and Pax wanted more than anything else to be healed.

"Let's go with him, Jayni," Pax said suddenly.

Jayni's eyes widened as she turned around to stare up at Pax. Pax—her friend who was always exhausted, who didn't want to do anything more daring than climb the first few limbs of their tree, whose sense of adventure had been lost ever since he got sick two years ago. This was the old Pax talking, and she liked it.

"Yes! Oh, Pax, let's do it! Let's go!"

"Quite right, then. You've finally come to your senses. Off we go," said Wilmer, turning toward the doorway and muttering. "This is a fine metal of fish, but Declan'll know what to do."

Kettle, thought Pax as he climbed down from his tree limb and stepped toward the black hole. *A kettle of fish.* He watched cautiously as the frazzled bird hopped through the opening. Then he watched in amazement as the black hole grew larger for Jayni, who stepped in behind Wilmer without hesitating.

Pax crept up to the very edge of the doorway. Peering in, he felt a blast of damp air hit his face. He could see nothing, but smelled a strong scent of dirt and rain. Pax stood motionless, except for his heart, which beat fast with both hope and fear. *A healing man. A healing man*, he silently repeated. He closed his eyes, forced his right foot forward, and stepped inside the oak tree.

2

The Mersades

Darkness seemed to swallow Pax. The hole behind him instantly closed, and he stretched out his hand to feel what was in front of him. His hand hit the back of Jayni's head.

"Ow!"

"Sorry. I can't see anything."

"Wilmer said to stay here for a minute and not to move," Jayni whispered.

The two children stood in silence, breathing in the muggy air and mustiness of the inner trunk. Pax could almost *feel* the darkness.

Then Wilmer's frenzied voice commanded, "Touch the walls!"

The children reached out to their right and to their left. But neither of them could feel anything.

Jayni carefully shuffled sideways, groping with her fingers till they hit something lumpy and spongy, like the tops of mushrooms packed tightly together. At her touch, the spongy lumps made the walls glow with a faint bluish-purple light. The light slowly moved over the cylindrical insides of the tree, around and under and over them. Jayni gasped with excitement and pressed both her hands hard against the spongy wall, which made the light glow brighter.

But Pax wasn't paying attention to the walls. He was staring over Jayni's shoulder at the steep staircase growing down like a root into the floor before them. Pax stepped around Jayni and watched as it unfurled downward, descending deep, deep into the ground, glowing like everything else. He timidly touched his right foot on the first step down. It was soft and springy. "Jayni, look."

The staircase was narrow, so Jayni squeezed past Pax on the first step and looked down. She burst out giggling. "Amaaazing!" She bounced down the next few steps. "It's like a trampoline staircase!"

Jayni stopped in her tracks when she saw Wilmer flutter-hopping up the steps toward her. His wattles swung wildly, his feathers looking even frowzier than before. With a dramatic wave of his wing, he called, "Come quickly! Follow me. We must find Declan."

He turned and began fluttering clumsily down the staircase, with Jayni a couple of steps behind him and Pax a few steps behind Jayni. Pax noticed that the farther down they went, the quieter everything became—as if the spongy, padded stairs and walls swallowed noises whole. Wilmer's directions to "Follow closely!" and "Keep touching the walls!" and "Don't bounce on the stairs!" sounded as if he were talking from inside a pillow.

Now the staircase began to twist like an S, curving down to the left, then around to the right, then back to the left, until it ended abruptly about fifteen minutes later. Three pitch-dark tunnels lay before them: two to their right, and one to their left.

Wilmer puffed up his chest, fluffed his wings, and said, "Left tunnel. No light. Hold on to the walls."

Jayni charged ahead, excited at every new aspect of this adventure, but Pax felt fear creeping up his spine. He hated the dark. He dreaded nighttime. In fact, he still slept with a little light on at night. With each step farther into this blind tunnel, his heart beat faster and his head pounded harder. Why hadn't he asked where they were going or what the way would be like? *But . . . what about the healer? Darkness is worth the chance to be healed,* Pax told himself. He began picturing himself with hair, running with his friends on the soccer field, eating food without getting sick. *I can do this*, he told himself, pulling back his shoulders and plodding on through the darkness.

The tunnel emptied into a large room—a room illuminated by that same bluish-purple light from the staircase. Branching off from this room were ten or fifteen more tunnels. Wilmer marched confidently to the fifth one from the right.

Pax quietly groaned. All his confidence seemed to disappear again. He leaned close to Jayni and whispered, "We'll never be able to find our way out of here."

"Maybe. But can you believe what's been inside our Climbing Tree all this time? *Amazing!*" she whispered back.

It didn't feel amazing to Pax. His labored breathing and sluggish steps reminded him that he was far too sick for an adventure like this—but there was no turning back now.

Just then, a small dot of light appeared in the distance, and with every step they took, it grew larger and brighter till it was a blinding light joined by a deafening sound—and then out they all stepped, onto a massive flat rock on the backside of a waterfall.

Pax at once forgot his fears. The rock they were standing on led them around the waterfall, which thundered from hundreds of feet above him and crashed like a million glistening diamonds into a little lake of foaming white, and then gently sloped into calmer turquoise water. On the far side of the lake purple pepper trees grew and silver lilies stood seven feet tall. Beyond that, a wide river flowed southeast. The sun burst low and brilliant, which made everything feel like early morning.

While Pax stood gaping at the spectacle, wondering how this enchanted world lay at the bottom of their Climbing Tree, Jayni slid down the wet, slick rock like a waterslide, landing with a splash in the cold knee-deep water. She threw her head back and opened her mouth wide to catch spray from the falls. She waded out even farther till the water was up to her waist, splashing and swimming till she was a happy, dripping mess.

When she paused to wring water out of her hair, she caught sight of Wilmer flying away—if it could be called flying. He thrashed wildly about, careened to the left, dropped dangerously close to the water, flapped back up with great effort—but slowly and awkwardly he was leaving the children behind.

Jayni yelled at him at the top of her lungs, but of course, not even the loudest of voices could be heard above the waterfall's roar. So, she jumped up and down and waved her arms frantically, but Wilmer was oblivious to it all. He flew farther and farther away, till he could not be seen at all.

Pax watched in horror. He sank down onto the rock and cradled his bald head in his hands. His shoulders slumped forward. His temples throbbed. *We shouldn't have come. Why did I get my hopes up? We're lost! How are we ever going to get back home?*

Fear grabbed Pax by his chest. He knew this feeling well. He always felt it at night when his parents walked out of his bedroom and the house fell quiet and he was alone with his thoughts. He felt it too in the hospital bed as bags of nauseating liquids dripped down plastic lines and into his chest. He felt it when kids at school stared at him—at his bald head, bony body, and the dark circles around his eyes.

Pax hated feeling afraid. But now he hated himself for caving to courage, for stepping into that tree, for jumping at the impossible hope of being healed. He wanted to cry and run and hide. *Why do so many bad things happen to me? My life is horrible.*

His thoughts were interrupted when he saw Jayni wading through the waist-high water to get to him, yelling words he couldn't understand and furiously pointing at

something. He followed her gaze and looked to his right. There in the distance was the silhouette of a ship sailing toward them on the river. Pax stood up, and both kids watched intently as the vessel drew nearer and nearer. And there on the tippy top of the tallest mast was . . . *Wilmer.*

Pax started breathing again.

Jayni scrambled up beside him where they both looked on in wonder as the ship sailed right up to the waterfall— just out of reach of the rock—then floated gently to a stop.

The ship was straight out of an adventure story: a multi-decked, dark-wooded vessel, with brightly colored sails and white twinkle lights hanging from her three masts. Her bow was carved with the face of a fierce snow leopard, and her name was painted on her port side in large gold letters: *Mersades.*

Wilmer flew haphazardly down to the children and alighted on the rock beside them. "Splickety-lit, here we are. She's a beauty, yes?"

The children were surprised to find they could hear Wilmer. The roar of the waterfall had been silenced. Both children looked at Wilmer in shock.

Pax asked, "How can we hear you now? What happened to the waterfall?"

"Well, well, it's one of many surprises that await you."

Wilmer motioned to the ship. "Wherever the Mersades goes, magic follows."

"Mer-say-deez," said Jayni slowly. "That's beautiful. But why is her masthead a leopard when she's a *sea* vessel?" asked Jayni. "Shouldn't she be a mermaid or something?"

Pax looked at her with a bit of surprise: he knew that Jayni was smart, but not *that* smart. How did she know what a masthead was?

"Quite right, quite right. Not a mermaid, to be sure. A snow leopard! Ha! Well, flummox me, it's a story worth telling—but I do seem to get all the details bungled up when I tell it. You'll have to ask Declan."

"Who *is* Declan?" asked Pax.

Wilmer cocked his head, as if considering whether—or maybe how—to answer. But he was quickly distracted when a short gangway appeared on the port side of the ship, unrolling like a carpet and resting on the edge of the rock just a few feet from them. He flapped his wings and cried, "Ah, she's ready! Spot-spit, up you go!"

"Wait!" said Pax. "How far is this ship going? We have to be home in an hour or our parents will worry."

Jayni quietly groaned at the thought of not boarding the beautiful vessel bound for adventure, but she had to agree with Pax—it would be crazy to sail away into the unknown without a way back home by dinnertime.

"Well, knock me down with my feathers. You two don't have a clue, do you?" said Wilmer. "I guess Declan will have to start with the basics. *Of course* you'll be home by dinner. Now, pick up your heels and follow me."

And with that, he waddled up the gangway, and the children followed him, desperately hoping they weren't making a mistake—but secretly tingling with excitement.

As quickly as it had appeared, the gangway disappeared behind them, and the children walked down three short steps to stand on the ship's deck. Around the perimeter of the deck was a bench full of cushions and cozy blankets and, here and there, breakfast trays with cups of steaming liquid. (Pax caught a whiff of it and knew it was something like hot cocoa.) At the far end of the deck, steps led up to the stern and captain's quarters, and steps led down to the crew's quarters and supply decks. Thick ropes hung like webs and golden railings blazed; a crow's nest crowned the top of the main mast and a gigantic wooden wheel steered the course.

As the children stood and stared, Wilmer flew to the tallest mast, calling down, "*I* am a three-wattled *bellbird*, so I don't sit in the *crow's* nest!" Then with a flourish of his right wing and much wattling of his wattles, he cried,

"Hoist the sails! Decks away!"

"I think he means 'anchors aweigh,'" Jayni whispered with a giggle.

3

The Nymph

When Wilmer ordered the sails to be hoisted, no one appeared. There was no captain. No crewmen, no deckhands. The sails simply raised themselves, caught wind, and set the ship into motion. Jayni ran to the back of the ship, up a few steps to the stern, and watched the waterfall disappear out of sight.

Pax settled onto the cozy bench on the port side of the ship, reeling from all the activity of the last two hours. He was almost delirious with exhaustion. He looked with longing at the cups of steaming drink.

Wilmer called down, "Well, well, plop a squat and help yourselves to the popple-cream. Do you have popple-cream where you're from?" Without waiting for their answer, Wilmer continued in the same breath, "Sailors used to drink it to calm their stomachs when the seas turned choppy, and it contains a secret ingredient, but I always forget if it's the nectar from the teazel herb or the snotty-gobbles tree. No matter. It's warm and soothing, just the thing for our journey. Snacks are coming shortly. I'm in over my beak with ship business, but Darya will be here soon."

Pax and Jayni's heads were spinning with questions. Jayni returned to the port side and sat beside Pax, and after they'd taken one sip of the popple-cream, all was momentarily forgotten. The drink was even better than the best hot cocoa back home—perfectly warm and choc-olaty, creamy with hints of vanilla and toasted almonds and . . . it had something else in it . . . something that made the children feel like it was summer vacation and Christ-mas all in one sip. It calmed Jayni's fidgety energy, and it soothed Pax's throat, raw from coughing.

After Pax drained his cup, he pulled a blanket around his shoulders, leaned back into the deep cushions, and fell asleep.

Jayni looked back up at Wilmer, then giggled to see him fast asleep—his black beak and wattles tucked into his right wing. She took a seat next to Pax, slowly sipping her drink and looking out at the passing scenery. The sky above them was covered in glossy, silvery clouds, as if they'd been briefly dunked in water and then hung to dry. On the distant horizon were blue mountains, but on either side of the ship, just a stone's throw away, was a thick wall of birch trees and cherry blossoms. The air felt cool and smelled sweet.

The water moved smoothly yet as swiftly as a river—slapping against the sides of the ship in rhythmic time—but the farther they sailed, the wider the water grew till it was no longer a river but an ocean, and the tree-lined banks faded far behind them.

Jayni was so mesmerized by it all that she didn't even notice when a beautiful creature materialized out of thin air and floated onto the deck. Moving and shimmering as if she were made of mist and light, she would have stood eye-to-eye with Jayni . . . if she'd had feet.

"Greetings," the wispy creature said gently.

Jayni almost dropped her drink at the sight of the enchanting being with satiny dark skin, even darker eyes, and hair made of stardust. She wore a delicate gown that looked as if it had been spun from silky cobwebs. She was possibly the most beautiful creature Jayni had ever seen.

"I'm Darya," said the creature in a voice that sounded like a wise and happy song.

"Oh . . . oh! I'm—I'm Jayni."

Darya smiled a smile that made her hair sprinkle star-dust and her eyes twinkle like stars.

"Dar-ee-yuh," said Jayni carefully, because she didn't like her own name mispronounced. "You're, who are . . . I mean, you are . . ."

"A nymph," finished Darya. She floated closer to Jayni.

Jayni stood up from her bench seat, never taking her eyes off Darya.

The nymph continued, "I'm here to help you along your way." (*Was she singing or speaking?* Jayni wondered.) "I've brought food for refreshment and supplies for the journey."

"Journey?" asked Jayni. "I actually don't know where we're headed or what we're doing. All I know is that my friend Pax and I came for adventure," she said with excitement in her voice. She looked at Pax who was still sleeping. "Well, I think Pax came because he wants to be healed."

"He's sick?" asked Darya, glancing at the sleeping boy.

"Yeah." Jayni's face clouded over. "*Really* sick. He has . . . cancer."

"What's cancer?" asked Darya.

"Oh! You don't know what cancer is?" asked Jayni, surprised. "It's a disease that can take over your body and even kill you. And to keep it from killing you, you have to take all kinds of medicine . . . stuff that makes you sick from head to toe. It's awful. Pax has been sick for two whole years, ever since we were eight."

"That's so sad," whispered Darya, her starry eyes filling with tears. "Is the medicine working?"

"I hope so," said Jayni. Then, her lip quivering, "I—I don't know." Her eyes became pools of saltwater as she glanced behind her at her sleeping friend.

"Oh, Lovie. My heart hurts for you. It must be terrible to watch your friend suffer so."

Jayni was quiet. She blinked away hot tears and tried to focus on Darya's glimmering face. Her voice trembled, "Everyone thinks Pax is so strong, so brave—and he *is*—but I think deep down he's scared. We've been friends all our lives, but whenever I ask him if he's scared or sad, he just stares at the ground and doesn't say anything." Jayni paused, then added, "I don't know how to help him."

Darya gently took Jayni's hand. "Sometimes sitting with a friend in their pain is the best way to care for them. Just being there. It sounds like you've been a good friend."

Jayni's eyes overflowed. "I hope so. I just feel bad 'cause secretly I like the old Pax better—the *healthy* Pax. Everything . . . changed. *He* changed."

The two fell silent. Jayni heard the lapping of ocean waves against the side of the ship and smelled the briny breeze caressing her face.

Darya asked, "What do you like most about your friend?"

Jayni's eyes brightened through her tears. "Pax is— well, *Pax!* He likes adventures as much as I do—well, at least he *used* to. He makes me laugh so hard. And he acts like my protector, like a big older brother, even though he was born three weeks *after* me. Like once, he saw a skunk that he thought was gonna spray me, so he yelled and chased it away, but the skunk got so scared, he sprayed Pax! He stunk for a whole week!"

Darya laughed with Jayni, and Pax began to stir.

"Well now, Lovie, you two must be starving. How about a snack?" asked Darya.

Jayni nodded eagerly.

Darya held out her hands, and instantly they were filled with a wooden tray overflowing with berries and nuts, chocolates and cheeses, candy popcorn, two tall glasses of sparkling water, and a jug filled with more steaming popple-cream.

Jayni cried, "It's all so pretty! Almost too pretty to eat— but I'll eat it anyway!" Then her face fell. "Pax can't eat most of these things. He gets really sick."

Darya smiled. "This food will not make him sick, I promise. It is pure, vibrant, living food, and he will feel stronger, not sicker, after eating it."

Pax sat up and looked first at Darya, then at her feast, then at Jayni. He blinked a few times. "Is it possible to dream a dream inside a dream?" he asked.

They all laughed, and Jayni said, "Pax, meet Darya. She is a . . . what was it? *Fairy?*"

"A nymph," laughed Darya. "Fairies are small and mischievous creatures. Nymphs are nurturing spirits who are as big as humans and love to sing and dance. I'm a celestial nymph." She shot into the air high above their heads, spinning and twirling like a ballerina—her hair showering down stardust, the sun glinting silver off her dress. She floated gracefully back down to the deck.

Jayni was enchanted. Beaming, she said, "Darya, meet my friend, Pax."

Pax began to stand up for introductions, but Darya motioned for him to stay seated. Jayni took a seat next to him.

To the children's left was the bow of the ship, which continued to forge ahead into the vast ocean. To their right was the stern of the ship, and if they looked straight ahead, out and over the deck, they saw nothing but jewel-blue water.

Darya hovered close with her tray of treats, and the three of them laughed and ate and drank and talked till the sky felt four-o'-clockish and the air grew cooler. The children weren't sure if it had been an hour or an entire day since they stepped into their Climbing Tree, but one thing was clear: time worked differently here—wherever *here* was.

Pax fought against a growing fear that they may have missed dinner hours ago, that their parents were frantically searching for their missing kids. *I probably napped for only a few minutes. Maybe there's a quick way back once we . . .*

His reasoning was interrupted by a frenzied voice overhead. "Laaand ajoy!"

The children glanced up to see Wilmer, feathers flapping, eyes bulging with excitement as he surveyed the horizon.

Darya called out, "Hello, my friend! As always, you are a delight."

"Ahhh, Darya! Brilliant, brilliant. Carry in, carry in!"

"Carry *on*, carry *on*," Darya said with a knowing wink at the children.

"Well, Lovies," Darya's tone turned serious. "We are nearing the Bay of the Bumfuzzles, where you will finally meet the wise and kind Declan. He will know how to help you best. But beware: the bay is named for the creatures who often roam the water's edge in search of new victims to bewitch. The Bumfuzzles have succeeded in distracting many a traveler from his course. They will succeed with you too unless you sing a song so sweet that it overpowers their wicked charms."

Darya held out her hands and produced a tiny scroll. Unrolling it, she sang in a lilting voice,

'Tis strongest love
To sing the truth
To one who errs
By lies uncouth.
Their freedom comes
In song, forsooth—
The music sets them free!

Pax and Jayni looked at each other, then back at the nymph.

"It's so beautiful . . . but I don't think we understand it," Jayni said.

"*At all,*" added Pax.

"Oh, of course you don't, Lovies. Not yet anyway. That is why you will take the scroll with you. When you unroll it, it will sing the song for you—but you must concentrate all your attention on its beauty and stop your ears to the noise of the Bumfuzzles."

Then Darya handed the scroll to Pax, saying, "Because you are a protector of friends."

Pax took the scroll with great solemnity and pride. He'd been sick for so long that he'd forgotten what it felt like to be entrusted with special responsibility.

Darya continued with her instructions. "Once the ship reaches shore, you'll see a flight of wooden steps tucked into a sandy bluff, at the top of which is a meadow. Pass through the meadow till you come upon a small bridge. Cross it without looking behind you, and you will be out of harm's way. The Bumfuzzles cannot cross that bridge. On the other side is the cottage of Declan. Go up to the door and knock three times."

"Then what will happen?" asked Pax.

"That is as much as I know," said Darya. "Just be sure to unroll the scroll at the first sign of a Bumfuzzle."

"What do the Bumfuzzles *look* like?" asked Jayni.

Darya answered, "The Bumfuzzles constantly change their form and habitat, so one never knows *what* they will look like. But underneath all their disguises are monstrous faces and beastly spirits."

Darya paused as she held out her hands and produced two leather satchels. "You need one more thing for your journey," she said as she handed a satchel to each child.

Pax lifted the flap of his satchel and peered inside. He found a seed the size of an almond, five green leaves, a black cloth, and a canteen that could hold no more than a sip of water.

Jayni was rifling through her satchel and finding the same items as Pax, except that instead of a seed, she had a tiny square-inch quilted blanket, just the right size for a dollhouse bed.

Darya warned them, "If the Bumfuzzles succeed in bewitching you, they will steal your satchels."

At the children's puzzled expressions, she explained, "It's the seed and the blanket they want."

"Why? What are they for?" asked Pax.

"It would make no sense to explain it all now, but when you need them, you will understand their importance," said Darya. "You *must not* let them fall into the hands of the Bumfuzzles."

The ship was now fast approaching land. Jayni looked left and gasped. She ran up to the bow for a better view. It was as if they'd sailed into a painting of Ireland. Beyond the shimmering bay were miles of emerald-green hills, and beyond those hills were snowcapped mountains set against a blue sky and billowing clouds. Everywhere they looked emerald-green yews, towering oaks, and papery-barked birches filled the landscape. The tiny purple blooms of dog violets and the white, sweet-scented flowers of honeysuckle bushes bordered ancient cobblestone paths that led to the doors of small cottages with thatched roofs and stone chimneys that blew wisps of smoke into the sky.

"Ohhhhhh . . . !" was all Jayni could manage to say.

Pax had followed her to the bow, with Darya right behind him. "Is this the Bay of the Bumfuzzles?" he asked.

"Indeed, it is! One of the most beautiful bays in all the world," said Darya. "It is cold here, but you will soon find warmth in the cottage of Declan. Come. The ship has docked and the gangway is ready." She led them down from the bow, across the deck, and to the unfurled bridge between the boat and a small sandy beach. "And now, Lovies, I must away. Godspeed, dear children."

For a moment the breathtaking view was forgotten as the three exchanged hugs and well wishes. Pax smiled—being hugged by a nymph was like being wrapped in the softest, lightest blanket in the world.

Wilmer suddenly popped up through a trap door on the deck and squawked, "Cheery-ah, friends! Cheery-ah!

Declan will put everything right!"

Darya gestured to the gangway, and with satchels strapped across their chests, Pax and Jayni disembarked. They took a few shuffling steps in the sand, then turned around to say one last goodbye—but to their surprise, Darya and Wilmer were nowhere to be seen, the sails were fast asleep, and all was still.

The children stared at each other with wide eyes.

"I keep thinking we're going to wake up and be so disappointed that this was all just a dream," said Jayni.

Pax reached over and gave Jayni's straight black hair a firm tug.

"Ow! What was that for?" she cried.

"Proof that it's not a dream," Pax teased.

Jayni rolled her eyes and pretended to be angry. She walked away from Pax toward a narrow flight of cobblestone steps that connected the sandy beach to a sprawling meadow of green clover. She started counting the steps as she always did back in her two-story home: "One, two, three, four . . ."

Pax smiled and moved slowly toward the steps, shivering from the cold that blew through his body like a knife through paper.

"Keep your eyes open for any dangerous creatures,

Spitfire," he called. "As soon as we see even one Bumfuzzle, we'll unroll the scroll before they have a chance to bewitch us."

"Yes, *Dad*," Jayni called over her shoulder. She kept counting as she climbed, "Nine, ten, eleven, twelve! Pax, twelve steps, just like at home! . . . Oh! How *adorable*!"

Pax was just beginning his ascent up the steps when he lost sight of Jayni. By the time he reached the top, breathless and curious, he saw her pointing at several small, dog-like animals with white fur, oversized ears, wide black eyes, and button noses.

"Aww, baby fennec foxes, Pax! My favorite animal ever! They are *so adorable*!"

"Maybe too adorable," Pax said cautiously. In fact, he'd never seen anything that cute in his life.

The fennec foxes—who seemed to be multiplying by the second—danced playfully around the children, yipping and blinking up at them with puppy eyes. They tumbled and rolled and cuddled with each other. The bolder ones let Jayni pet them; the quieter ones sat at Pax's feet, as if they knew he was too weak to play. Jayni started plotting how she could take one home as a pet.

But as Pax continued to watch them, his caution turned into concern. A couple of the foxes were smiling—a forced half-smile that pulled their lips tight against jagged teeth. Just to be safe, he pulled out the scroll, ready to release its song at any moment.

"Jayni, be careful. These may be Bumfuzzles."

"There's no way, Pax." Jayni's voice sounded almost shrill as her excitement rose. "Look at these fluffy white fur babies!"

One of the foxes stared up at Jayni and asked in a tiny, high-pitched voice, "Are you a princess?"

A second one bowed low and tittered, "Your majesty."

A third one squeaked, "At your service!"

Before the children had entered the Climbing Tree, they would have been scared to death to hear an animal speak, but now, after spending the day with a talking bird and a beautiful nymph, their shock was short-lived.

Jayni giggled. "I *wish* I was a princess!"

"You're as beautiful as a princess," one piped.

"*Just* like a princess," another purred.

The first baby fennec fox turned and pointed the curved claw of his fuzzy paw at the nearest cottage. "Come, Princess!"

Suddenly Pax knew. Maybe it was their smiles or their claws—or just an instinct—but Pax knew the foxes were all wrong. He quickly unrolled his scroll and immediately a beautiful voice began to sing words that floated off the page and into the air.

'Tis strongest love

To sing the truth . . .

The baby foxes' ginormous ears began to twitch. Their eyes flashed. With urgency in their squeaky voices, they almost pleaded with Jayni—

"Come, beautiful Princess!"

"Come quickly!"

"A warm cottage with yummy food!"

Jayni followed the baby foxes happily. As she did, more and more kits appeared from behind bushes and rocks and trees, joining in the squeaky chatter about how much Jayni looked and walked and sounded like a princess.

Pax groaned as he tried to keep up with Jayni while holding the scroll high over his head so that she might hear the scroll's song above the foxes' din—

Their freedom comes

In song . . .

"Jayni! Darya didn't say anything about following foxes! Something's not right . . ."

With sparkling eyes and a bounce in her step, Jayni glanced back at Pax. She felt a brief pang of guilt at the sight of his shivering body and pale face, but the baby fennec foxes enticed her, saying, "You are very welcome to share our warm fire and food, Your Highness!"

Being mistaken for a princess was possibly the single greatest moment of Jayni's life thus far. She looked back toward the foxes, telling herself that fire and food was just what Pax needed. She followed the foxes up to the cottage door, which appeared to swing wide on its own.

The foxes hesitated until Jayni stood right before the open door and then surrounded her, their furry tails clutching at her legs.

"They're adorable, Pax! Harmless! Stop being a killjoy and come on!"

Pax held the singing scroll high overhead with one hand and stretched the other hand toward Jayni, but his friend was beyond his reach. "Jayni, they're Bumfuzzles!" he cried.

Just as Jayni was bustled through the doorway, she shot a worried look over her shoulder at Pax.

Then the door slammed shut, and Jayni was gone.

4

The Cottage

Pax ignored the cold and pain that tore at his body as he charged for the door. He jiggled the handle. Locked.

He banged on the heavy, wooden door. He knocked louder.

Not a word or yip sounded from the other side.

Pax ran to the window beside the door, fighting for air as his chest heaved and rattled. He pressed his face to the glass, but could only make out a dark, empty room.

"Jayni!" he shouted. "Jaaayniii!" He circled the cottage, searching, knocking on walls and windows, and shouting.

Silence answered.

Why would she follow them?

Pax's body shook with spasms of coughing. He was mad. And scared. But he was too tired to keep up the search. He had to find the cottage of Declan before his body caved to the cold. He would get help and come back for Jayni.

Trembling, wheezing, and half-blinded by the icy wind, he turned back to the cobblestone path that ran through the middle of the village. He took a few steps onto the path, and his right foot caught the corner of a stone. Pax pitched forward, and all went black.

Pax awoke to the smell of apple cider and maple syrup. He was lying on his back atop something soft. Within arm's reach overhead, a thatched ceiling hung so low he knew he'd never be able to stand up. To his left, a fire blazed in a small stone fireplace; to his right sat a little wooden bed and an equally little, but old, travel trunk.

His head butted up against a drafty window, and his feet were sticking through a doorway into another room from which he heard a *thunk, thunk, clang, thunk, tap, tap, ting!*

A rosy, wrinkled face popped through the doorway. "Oh, yer awake, lad! Wonderful!"

Out hobbled a small man, no more than three feet tall,

with ruddy skin and a white beard that hung to his waist. He had a peg leg and wore brown knickerbockers with suspenders. His shirt was coarse and green with patches at the elbows, and a tweed scally-cap sat askew on his head.

"Almost suppertime! Ye warm now? Aye, there's more color in yer face. Good. Ye rest awhile longer, and I'll call ye when the food's ready."

He *thunk-thunked* back to the kitchen and began to hum a tune in chesty tones.

Pax was frantic to figure out what he was doing here. Like a film on fast-forward, his mind played images of a waterfall, a ship, a feast, a nymph, a shimmering bay, and—*Jayni!*

Pax sat bolt upright, his head just inches now from the ceiling, as the awful truth struck his heart. Jayni had been taken by the Bumfuzzles, and he had—left her? Gotten lost? Fallen! Yes, he remembered now the *thwack* of cobblestone against his forehead. His hand reached up to feel a sizeable goose egg on his temple.

But how had he ended up *here*? He had to find out fast and get back to Jayni as soon as possible.

The house, which was perfectly suited to a tiny man, made it impossible for Pax to stand up—or move around without bumping into something. So, he carefully shifted onto all fours, which gave him a throbbing sensation in his forehead. He crawled forward and stuck his head around the wall into the kitchen.

Everything was miniature in here too: a fireplace with a blazing fire, over which hung a steaming black pot; a few crooked but clean cupboards on the walls; and a rough wooden table with three stools.

"Yer up! Good, good. Ye hungry? One last dash of teazel, a pinch of gorse bush powder, and we'll eat!" said the man.

How food could smell that good when it had something called gorse bush in it, Pax could not fathom. But he was hungry enough to eat anything. However, first things first—

"Um, sir . . . I'd love to stay and eat, but I *have* to go find my friend. She was taken captive by the Bumfuzzles—I'm not sure if it was today or yesterday or how long ago. But I have to find her before—" His usual fit of coughing interrupted him and sent a shooting pain through the tender lump on his forehead.

"Ye say the Bumfuzzles took her captive?" asked the man after Pax's fit had passed.

Pax took a steadying breath. "Well . . . not *exactly*. They tricked her with a bunch of cute talk and princess stuff. It all happened so fast, and she followed them right into their cottage and then . . . disappeared!"

A grave look came over the little man's face. "I'm all too familiar with the Bumfuzzles and their trickery. I was one of their victims too, a very long time ago. Ye must have used a strong kind o' magic to keep their power from working on ye?"

"Yes, sir. A nymph, she gave me a scroll that sings a song. I don't understand what it means, but it worked. Jayni . . . my friend . . . I don't think she wanted to listen to it. She was listening to *them*. Now *please*, would you help me find her?"

"Ah, Darya. O' course. She is a dear friend o' mine, wise and kind. I'm so happy ye met 'er."

The little man dipped his ladle into the pot on the fire and brought it back to his lips, blowing and slurping its contents. "Mmm! My mother's recipe." He paused, ladle in midair, then nodded thoughtfully. "Yes, o' course, we will go get yer friend. But first, we must eat. And before that, we must introduce ourselves: me name is Declan. Welcome to me humble home. I had a li'l trouble draggin' ye in here, but nuthin' like the time I rescued a giant. Her foot was the only thing that would fit inside me door, and it musta weighed a hundred pounds all on its own!"

Pax could not believe what he was hearing. Jayni was in

great danger, and this man was prattling on about recipes and giants! Well, he would rescue Jayni himself then. He looked around for the front door, ignoring his rumbling tummy and rattling lungs.

Declan filled two soup bowls and set them on the table. Then his voice dropped deeper, and he frowned.

"Lad, we will not find Jayni back at that cottage. She will be miles from here by now, in Phantom Forest, where the Bumfuzzles make their nests and practice their dark deceivery. They have dug tunnels all o'er the countryside, secret passages into the forest. I can only assume that the cottage ye saw hides one o' their entrances. I will take ye there meself, and we will get 'er back. But first ye must eat. No good soldier fights on an empty stomach."

Declan took his seat on a three-legged stool, and Pax reluctantly crawled to the table, wondering, *Does everyone here feed you before sending you on a dangerous journey?* But as he sat cross-legged and took his first sip of warm soup—the most comforting soup he had ever tasted due to the coconutty gorse bush seasoning—and shoved a bite-sized maple syrup muffin into his mouth, he was glad they did.

The Hobblechaun

It was twilight when the pair finally left the shoebox of a cottage. Declan carried only a gnarled walking stick with a bulbous top that he could easily rest his chin upon. Pax wore a pair of boots, a beanie, and a wool jacket, all of which had magically been tailored to his exact size when Declan pulled them out of his travel trunk. After he had fully dressed, Pax slung Darya's satchel across his chest.

"Follow closely, lad," Declan said, as he began to weave his way through the thick ferns and grasses that grew behind his home. Cottages only dotted the landscape of this countryside—Declan's nearest neighbor was a mile away—so the world felt still and quiet as they stepped out onto a narrow dirt path that headed north, taking them farther away from the bay behind them.

The two made a funny pair—a skinny bald boy with a rattling cough, and a short, bearded man with a wooden leg. They walked along in silence as the sun snuffed out its light and left behind a periwinkle sky studded with stars. Their three feet and wooden leg made a rhythmic *cruffle-cruffle, shuffle-thunk* on the dirt path.

Pax cleared his throat. "Mr. Declan, do you mind my asking—are you a dwarf?"

Declan threw back his head and laughed like a pot bubbling over. "No, son. I'm a Hobblechaun—part hobbit, part elf, part leprechaun. I'm a rare breed. There are fewer than a hundred of us left in the world today, and most ne'er venture outside the enchanted hills o' Marion."

Pax was glad Declan couldn't see the goofy grin that lit up his face. All the stories he'd ever read about hobbits, elves, and leprechauns were rolled up into one magical creature called a Hobblechaun? It was enough to make a tired, anxious boy feel almost giddy.

"Is that where you're from? Marion?" asked Pax.

"Aye, it is. It's one o' the most beautiful places on earth, if I may say so meself."

Pax breathed a quiet sigh of relief. *At least I know we're on the same planet.*

It was dark now, but a quarter moon and a few bright

stars shone just enough light for the pair to see the path before them. All around them, the hills and trees became silhouettes against the night sky. Occasionally, an owl hooted or a cricket chirped.

"Why did you leave then?"

"More than one reason. Hobblechauns are charmin' folk—all wit and whimsy—but they're also greedy and lazy as the day is long. I wanted somethin' more than a comfortable home in a hill, a pot o' gold, and vacations in the North Pole. But, it was mostly this leg that made me leave." Declan tapped the peg with the bottom end of his walking stick. "And please, lad, call me Declan. No sir or mister."

Before Pax could ask him about his leg, Declan's cheery voice turned serious.

"Now, lad, when we reach the thicket ahead, we must go softly. We're travelin' by night because the Bumfuzzles love their sleep even more than they love the sound o' their own voices. They believe a long deep sleep keeps 'em young and charmin', so every night they sip the nectar o' the aphotic flower and sleep as hard as bricks fer ten straight hours. As long as we go quietly, they'll ne'er know we were there. But we'll have to hurry—they wake with the first light o' dawn."

Pax's chest heaved and rattled with a cough. He groaned. "Oh, no. My cough will give us away for sure."

"I'd almost forgotten," Declan said, coming to a halt. "Take out one o' the leaves from yer satchel."

Pax reached into his bag, wondering how a leaf had anything to do with his croupy chest.

"Chew it slowly as we walk. It won't cure anything, but it will quiet yer lungs fer a while."

Pax put the leaf in his mouth, bit down, and frowned— it was like chewing a banana peel. But there was no time for complaining. A solid wall of trees seemed to rise out of nowhere, blocking out the light of the moon and stars, shrouding them in utter darkness.

Declan tapped his walking stick three times, and Pax's eyes grew wide as he watched the top third of the stick glow with the light of a hundred fireflies. By this light, the two travelers stepped into the thick black forest.

Neither one said a word for half an hour as they ducked under low-hanging branches and dodged boulders and potholes along the path. Pax's eyes adjusted to the dim light of the firefly staff, and his chest wasn't rattling with coughs for the first time in months. But the farther they walked, the more his fear grew. He pulled his wool jacket tighter around him as strange sounds emanated from the woods, and his chest constricted as he thought more about confronting the Bumfuzzles. *How will we win Jayni back?* He was sick and weak, and Declan was not exactly the superhero type, plus the Bumfuzzles far outnumbered them.

Declan held up his hand and pointed to his left. "Here," he whispered.

Pax looked around but saw only the dark shapes of trees and bushes.

Declan handed Pax the staff, stepped into the brush, and pulled aside a curtain of prickly branches.

"Mmmph!" he grunted as a branch sprung back and snatched at his beard, catching it in its claw. Declan disentangled himself, then continued pulling and tugging at the plants, till Pax could see a hole in the hillside.

Pax quietly groaned. "A cave?"

Declan nodded.

Pax took a deep breath. Another dark tight space, like the tree trunk. Like the forest path.

Declan stepped in with ease, but once again Pax had to duck his head and squat. The chewing leaf was almost gone, and his lungs were back to rattling. He wasn't sure which fear was stronger—the thought of waking the Bumfuzzles or suffocating to death in a cave.

Jayni! Look at the mess you've gotten me into! But then a different thought made him panic. *What if I can't find her? What if I've lost my friend forever? What if we can't get back home and . . .*

Pax's thoughts yo-yoed as Declan reached back for the branches, pulling them back into place to hide the entrance.

Suddenly, there was a swishing sound and a bright light came on.

Pax covered his eyes.

"You made it!" said a hushed voice.

Pax squinted till his eyes could adjust. Then they bulged wide at the sight of Wilmer, the three-wattled bellbird, and Darya, the celestial nymph, glowing like a silvery moon in her gossamer gown.

Darya floated over to Pax and kissed him on the head. "I'm so happy you made it!" She took Pax's hands in hers. "And I'm sorry about Jayni. We're going to help you find her, Lovie."

Wilmer ruffled his wings, shook his wattles, and declared, "Those blasted Bumfuzzles! They're a laughing shame, the whole lot of them! They drive me up the door!" Wilmer began to pace back and forth, his wattles whirling, feathers twitching. "This time those scalawags have chewed off more than they can bite. They'll be sorry they messed with Jayni when they see *us* coming!"

He fluffed his feathers and opened his beak as if ready to sound his bell call, which elicited frantic hushing and shushing from the others.

"Now, Wilmer," chided Darya. "You know that the best way to get Jayni back is to catch the Bumfuzzles off guard. We don't want them to see us coming. Tonight, we need wisdom and patience."

"Quite right, quite right," he squawked, which was the closest he could come to whispering. "But if I hear even one peep out of those furry nincompoops, I'm gonna give them a piece of my brain!"

"Ye will not give them a piece of your mind," said Declan. "That's not part o' the plan."

Wilmer wasn't offended by Declan's correction. He was just happy to have gotten things off his chest. He shook his wattles, then sat down with an air of great satisfaction.

"All right, friends. As ye know, some of the Bumfuzzles are scattered in underground dens throughout the forest, but most of them hide in pocket caves on the northern cliffs," said Declan. "Every detail o' our plan is crucial in rescuin' Jayni and gettin' out alive. Let's review it all with Pax 'fore we set out."

The Rescue

The air had grown much colder by the time they all exited the cave an hour later, and Pax guessed it was well past midnight. He pushed his hands deep into the pockets of his jacket and chided himself for not having asked Declan about how time worked here. Did it pass differently than back home? It seemed that the farther into this world he traveled, the greater the differences felt. But now was not the time to ask questions. Silence was crucial.

Declan carefully covered the cave entrance once more and took a deep breath. He motioned to Pax to grab another chewing leaf for the way and exchanged wordless glances with the others that said, "Let's go get her."

Darya floated like a will-o'-the-wisp between the trees, while Wilmer fluttered from branch to branch above them.

Declan and Pax chose their steps carefully as they walked on the crunchy forest floor in the light of the firefly stick.

The way was uphill, and the trees were so close together that they seemed to be linking arms. Here and there was a fallen log, a rock, a prickly weed that clawed at ankles.

Pax silently fought against the aches and pains that tore at his body—and the fear that pounded at his heart.

Keep going . . . keep going . . . he chanted to himself.

There were strange sounds in this Phantom Forest: rustling, scampering, and howls that sent shivers down Pax's spine. If he'd been here alone, he would have fainted with fright, but traveling with a band of magical creatures gave him just enough courage for each next step.

The four rescuers progressed in this way for the better part of an hour, and then the trees thinned and gave way and exposed a sharp cliff ahead.

Everyone knew what to do. Declan tapped the firefly stick two times on the ground to darken it. Pax reached into his satchel and pulled out the black cloth, somehow knowing as soon as his fingers touched it what it would do. It was the size of a napkin and felt like cotton balls, light and soft and springy. Darya took hold of her silvery, weblike skirt and pulled and stretched it into a hammock of sorts—large enough to fit a full-grown adult. Wilmer flew up and over the cliff's edge, swooped down and out of sight, then circled back up and rejoined his friends. His eyes flashed in the sliver of moonlight.

Before Wilmer could say anything, Pax set the cloth on his head and it grew to cover him, making him silent and invisible. Everyone else ducked in along with him—the cloth growing larger and larger—till all four friends were safely hidden from prying eyes and ears. It was cramped and stuffy under the cloth, but it gave them a few protected moments to hear from Wilmer.

"The Bumfuzzles are there all right," said Wilmer with feathers twitching and wattles wagging. "Little pocket caves all up and down the cliff, and all of them sleeping soundly disguised as cute little foxes. Makes my mud boil." His voice changed from disgust to determination. "Jayni is pancaked between five or six Bumfuzzles in a cave about forty feet below."

Pax crinkled his forehead. "What do you mean? Is she all right?"

"*Sandwiched* between 'em," Declan translated. "All right then. Pax, are ye ready?"

Pax took a deep breath and slowly nodded. Without being told, he reached for another chewing leaf—he had two left now.

"Remember, once Darya has lowered ye down to the cave, ye must crawl in and wake Jayni ever so quietly. The Bumfuzzles are deep sleepers, but with Jayni in between two o' them, we're pushin' our luck. If they stir—Wilmer, you know what to do. I will be at the top o' the cliff, holding up the firefly stick. When Jayni is safely in Darya's net, fly her to the light."

Everyone was silent for a split second, knowing that this perfectly crafted plan could go very wrong if even one mistake was made. Then Declan held his firefly staff high over his head, and they all flew into action.

Pax grabbed a corner of the concealing cloth—which instantly shrunk back to size—then shoved it into his satchel. Darya floated upward a few feet, stretched herself out, and hovered parallel to the ground, causing her shimmering skirt-hammock to swing open for Pax.

He clumsily climbed then fell into it, but it was soft and springy and swung back and forth gently. He trembled so violently that his teeth chattered, and he fought back the urge to vomit. The last time he had felt this scared was in the hospital, being rolled into that operating room, all those bright lights and cold tubes and stinging needles. He'd known the game plan back then too—surgery. And just as he had then, he felt like a thousand other kids could do it better than he could—they could face danger and pain and the unknown without this paralyzing fear. But he looked up into Darya's fearless eyes, and with one hand clutching the satchel across his chest and one hand clinging to the skirt-hammock, he nodded that he was ready to go.

Darya nodded back at him and smiled in encouragement as she lifted him up and carried him to the edge of the cliff. Wilmer flew ahead of them, and Declan hobbled behind with the firefly stick glowing twice as brightly as before. They would need that light more than ever now because fog, like a thousand white snakes, slithered in from every corner of the mountain.

Wilmer circled the cliff two times, then dropped forty feet below, silently perching on a branch that stuck straight out of the mountainside. Eyes bulging more than usual, he lifted his left wing to point toward a shadowy recess in the rocks just beyond him. (Even in the terror of this moment, Pax was amused to see how stealthy and quiet the chatterbox bird could be.)

Darya deftly lowered her skirt-hammock as close to the cave as possible, and Pax caught his first glimpse of Jayni. She was indeed surrounded by Bumfuzzles, curled up on her side, only her head protruding from a white blanket of fluffy ears and tails. The cave was no bigger than a bathtub, so Jayni could easily be reached if only Pax could grab onto something to steady the swaying hammock.

He shimmied up onto his knees and reached as far as he could without tipping overboard, then he stretched out his left hand to grip a rock jutting out of the cave entrance. His heart was beating like a drum, and his mouth was painfully dry. Mustering every last ounce of energy and courage, he reached forward with his right hand and touched Jayni's head.

But as he did, the rock he was holding on to came loose and made a crumbling, cracking sound.

One of the Bumfuzzles stirred.

Panicked, Pax jumped back into the middle of the hammock, causing it to swing like a pendulum away from the cave entrance.

The Bumfuzzle rolled over, and Pax realized with relief that it was still asleep. But the swinging hammock headed back toward the cave and hit the edge of the opening with the force of Pax's body.

The fox's eyes cracked open. They bulged and flashed red at the sight of Pax, who had caught hold of another rock and steadied himself.

Jayni was stirring but not yet fully awake, and Pax knew they had no time to lose. He tugged on Jayni's hair. "Get up!" he commanded.

Jayni was still in a stupor, but she knew Pax's face and obeyed his voice. She scrambled to her knees and crawled toward the edge of the cave as Pax almost screamed, "You need to jump—*now*!"

Jayni, finally fully awake, took Pax's extended hand, holding tightly to the edge of the cave with her other hand. The first Bumfuzzle was already in motion, fangs suddenly jutting out of his mouth as he snapped at Pax's hand. A second Bumfuzzle had awoken and jumped onto Jayni's back, shrieking for its fellow Bumfuzzles to wake from their dens and join in the attack.

As they shrieked, the Bumfuzzles were contorting into something hideous: not only did their mouths sprout fangs, but their button noses turned bulbous, their eyes sank deep into their faces, their backs hunched, and their paws stretched into gnarled claws.

All of this seemed to happen in a matter of seconds. Somehow in the chaos, with ghoulish creatures clawing and biting and shrieking at her, Jayni let go of the rock she'd been holding on to, grabbed the edge of the hammock, and felt Pax pull her in beside him. She tumbled headfirst, crashing into Pax and causing the hammock to swing wildly in the air.

They could feel Darya fighting with all her might to steady them, before she quickly began her ascent back to Declan.

All over the cliff, dens came to life with an explosion of adorable-foxes-turned-Bumfuzzles. They bounded up the rocks like grotesque monkeys, hopping, clawing, skittering just yards beneath the children as Darya continued to rise. The fierce look in their eyes told the children they weren't going to give up easily.

Darya flew with her back to the sky, her eyes fixed on the children below her. Up and up she went. As soon as the three of them had passed the cliff's edge, she stopped her ascent with a jerk.

Pax searched desperately for the light of Declan's firefly stick in the thick fog that had gathered, knowing Darya too could see nothing.

The Bumfuzzles began to launch themselves from the cliff edge, grabbing at the bottom of the hammock.

Another jolt, and Darya flew headfirst, and out of reach, into the misty white blanket above them.

The children huddled together against the clinging cold and fright.

As Darya flew parallel to the ground at the top of the cliff, she called out for Declan. But her voice was lost in the thick fog and the shrieking of Bumfuzzles. She called again, but nothing. She carefully lowered her skirt-hammock until the children touched down onto wet grass and the hammock fell limp beneath them.

Pax and Jayni scrambled up. If they could have seen it, they would have marveled at how the hammock retracted into Darya's gown as if it had never existed. But no one could see a thing, and the children stretched out their arms to locate each other. Darya was shouting, "The Bumfuzzles are at our heels! Hold on!"

The three grabbed hands, making a kind of daisy chain. They rushed in the direction of the forest, Darya floating just above the ground while Jayni and Pax ran as fast as they could.

The fog was growing brighter around them, so they knew dawn was breaking. This meant the Bumfuzzles who made their dens in the forest would be awake now and ahead of them. And the Bumfuzzles from the cliffside dens had crested the edge of the cliff and were pursuing them from behind. The secret cave was their only chance of escape. They could only hope that Declan and Wilmer would have considered the same thing and would meet them there.

But now exhaustion and hunger and the cold, wet air began to take their toll on Pax's body. His lungs heaved and his flesh blazed with fever. Jayni felt Pax grow heavier with each step, and she had to pull with all her might to keep up with Darya while still holding on to him.

Finally, Jayni yelled "Stop!" and let go of Darya's hand. Pax had slumped to the ground, wracking with coughs, gasping for breath. Jayni dropped to her knees and cradled his head in her hands.

"He's burning up!" she cried to Darya. "Pax, hang on! I'm so sorry! This is all my fault."

For the first time, she noticed what Pax was wearing and quickly, carefully began removing the beanie from his head, the satchel from his chest, and the heavy wool jacket from his body. Darya floated close beside her and ran her fingers through her hair, gathering a handful of stardust that she lightly sprinkled on Pax's forehead and chest. Next, she went to work stretching and wrapping her enchanted skirt around him like a cocoon. When he was securely tucked in, she lifted him into her arms.

"This stardust swath will keep the fever down—for a while," Darya explained. "But we can't go to the cave now. We'll have to take the way around the mountain."

Jayni heard something in Darya's voice that told her the way around the mountain was also the dangerous way.

Darya turned east, heading on a path away from both

the forest and the cliffs, into the face of the rising sun, which had just broken through the fog. Before Jayni ran after her, she scooped up Pax's satchel, which she'd left on the ground. Her heart dropped as she suddenly realized she no longer had her own satchel. The Bumfuzzles had taken it, just like Darya had said they would.

How could I have been so blind, especially after Darya warned me? Pax did too.

The Bumfuzzles had flattered her, captured her, and pelted her with questions about a magic seed and a miniature blanket. They'd dragged her through that dreadful forest and forced her to drink a sickeningly sweet syrup.

She couldn't remember anything after that. She would still be unconscious and captive if Pax hadn't risked his own life to save hers.

Jayni sprinted to catch up with Darya. But as light as her feet were, her heart was that much heavier. She had ruined everything. Ruined an adventure with Pax. Ruined his chance at getting healed. Now he was sicker than ever, thanks to her selfishness. They were so far off course, they may never find their way home. Sadness heaved like a boulder onto her chest. Maybe this was how Pax felt when he struggled to breathe.

Darya had put distance between the three of them and

the Bumfuzzles, but now Jayni heard another sound: a wild flapping and muttering above them. She scanned the clearing and brightening sky for a glimpse of—yes, it was—*Wilmer*! The bellbird was flying almost directly above her now, and in his talons was a tiny man with a wooden leg and a glowing walking stick.

Jayni and Darya cried with joy as they watched Wilmer lower Declan onto a large, flat rock just ahead of them. Declan was wind-blown and wild-eyed, but he quickly recovered when he saw Pax wrapped up in Darya's arms.

"What happened?" he asked, hopping off the rock and hobbling over to meet Jayni and Darya who had finally slowed to a stop. Wilmer fluttered close behind him.

"It was too much for him," Darya said softly.

Jayni stood beside her, fighting back more tears.

"We're taking Pax to see *him*," Darya added, in a tone half fearful, half hopeful. "So, we have to go around the mountain."

"Wow, there. Hold your ponies! What?" exclaimed Wilmer.

"It's too soon. That's far too risky," Declan said.

"I know," said Darya. "But it's his only chance, Declan. You know the other way would be a week's journey."

"He may not choose to heal 'im, Darya," Declan warned.

"Yes," she answered, "but Pax will meet him, and that will be enough. You know that better than anyone."

They're taking Pax to the healing man, Jayni thought. *But what do they mean he might not heal Pax?*

Jayni looked at Pax's limp body and suddenly found herself speaking her secret thoughts aloud.

"The healing man just *has* to heal Pax. He just *has* to!" Embarrassed by her outburst, and on the verge of tears again, she hung her head and wrung her hands.

Declan hobbled over to Jayni. Even though he was a foot shorter than she, he spoke to her with the warmth and tenderness of a grandfather.

"Dear one, I am Declan. And ye must be Jayni."

Jayni nodded. *The cottage of Declan,* she thought. She liked this wee man's cheery face and the lilt of his warm voice.

He smiled and his kind eyes crinkled. "Lass, I've been eager to meet ye. Your friend Pax cares a great deal for ye, and I can tell ye care for 'im likewise." Declan paused and adjusted the tweed scally-cap on his head. "Are ye ready to face some more danger to help 'im?"

Jayni realized this gentle stranger knew about her horrible failure, yet he spoke to her as a friend. Her heart filled with hope for both Pax and herself.

"Yes! Yes, I'm ready!"

Declan turned to Wilmer. "I hate the idea as much as ye do, ol' friend—but I'm in need o' another lift."

"Oh, yes. Why of course, Declan, no trouble at all. For Pax. Might as well kill two stones with one bird, I always say," prattled Wilmer.

7

The Legend of Zade

The sun shone directly overhead when the five travelers stopped to rest. It was hot, and the road had turned increasingly steep and narrow over the last hour. To their right lay a wall of jagged boulders, as long and high as sleeping giants. To their left, the ground dropped straight down to a gray valley a mile below. Jayni glanced down once and almost fainted. From then on, she kept one hand on the rocks and her eyes fixed on Darya who glided in front of her.

The traveling party of five had outpaced and outwitted the Bumfuzzles by avoiding the forest completely and moving through a broad wasteland before beginning their climb up and around the rocky mountain. The Bumfuzzles could not tolerate bright light and heat. They'd eventually given up their pursuit and shrunk back into the recesses of the dark forest.

Jayni was exhausted and hungry. Famished. And so thirsty her mouth seemed coated in desert sand. She looked up at Declan who was wiggling uncomfortably in Wilmer's grasp. They both looked grumpy, and she knew for a fact that Wilmer was exhausted because he hadn't said one word for at least half an hour. Even Darya seemed to be fading—her stardust hair looked more like chalk dust, and her once-radiant gown hung limp and dull.

Pax still lay motionless in her arms, except for an occasional short raspy gasp, followed by a long gravelly exhale. Each time, the sound made Jayni's heart drop, but it also reassured her that Pax was still alive.

Just as they felt they could go no farther, the travelers spied a patch of dry grass ahead, in the shade of a giant boulder. Without a word, everyone stumbled toward it. Jayni dropped to the ground, and Darya gently laid Pax (still swaddled in the folds of her gown) beside her. Wilmer came in for a bumpy landing, and Declan's wooden leg flung up dust and pebbles as he tumbled.

As everyone caught their breath, Darya admitted, "I can't seem to be able to make a full meal for us, but perhaps these small morsels will help."

She handed each one a giant fig and a few walnuts.

Declan asked Jayni to look in Pax's satchel. "Is the canteen still in there?"

Jayni dug around inside the satchel and pulled out the tiny, round leather container.

"Drink, dear one—drink till yer not thirsty anymore."

Jayni raised her eyebrows. One gulp of water was *not* going to quench her fierce thirst. She wanted to guzzle a *gallon* of water. Ice cold water. But she put the canteen to her lips and drank anyway.

And drank.

And drank.

It was the purest water she had ever tasted, and it kept flowing till she felt perfectly satisfied.

Then Declan asked, "May I?"

"Of course!" said Jayni as she handed the canteen to him, her eyes bright with awe.

Declan drank till his thirst was quenched, then passed it along to Wilmer, who clenched it in his beak and drank till he too was satisfied.

As the company rested in the shade, Jayni thought back to the ship *Mersades*. It was a happy memory—before everything had gone wrong. "Declan, when we were on the *Mersades*, Wilmer said you could tell me the story of the snow leopard . . . you know, the ship's masthead?"

Declan smiled, and a faraway look came into his eyes. "Mmm. Aye, the snow leopard. Well, I s'pose a few minutes' more rest will do us good. The hardest part of the journey is ahead, and we'll need our strength."

Despite their exhaustion, Darya's eyes sparkled, and Wilmer fluffed his feathers in excitement—

"This story is better than *The Tortoise and the Mare*!"

Declan chuckled, then began . . .

"Hundreds o' years ago, a man seized rule of this land— a man who drew his seemingly limitless powers from some unseen source. He could run faster, fight harder, and think smarter than the best in the land. Sadly, he grew selfish and arrogant and used his powers fer evil, surroundin' himself with liars, thieves, and goons."

"Some say the goons are the ancestors of the Bumfuzzles!" interrupted Wilmer.

Declan sighed and gave Wilmer a wilting look.

"Right! I'll zip my teeth."

Declan continued. "When the citizens o' the land spoke out against the wicked lord, he raised up an army to squelch their rebellion. From then on, anyone who refused to join in his evil ways was cruelly punished. The air turned foul, and even the sun's light dimmed in the shadow of his reign. The soil stopped producing good food and instead grew brambles, thorns, and thistles.

"But among the people there lived a few courageous ones who refused to be intimidated by the evil tyrant and his officers. They loved their land that had once been full o' peace and beauty, and more than that, they loved the true lord o' the land, Zade, who was believed to have been killed when the evil lord stole the throne. Zade had promised that an even greater ruler than himself was comin', one who would take away all the pain and sadness in life. Even though a cruel lord had overtaken the land instead o' the promised great one, these people still chose to believe Zade, and live as he had lived—loving and hoping and giving.

"The evil lord and his band of evildoers tracked down every last one of Zade's courageous followers, locked 'em in the hull of a ship, and sent it off to sea. *That would be a slow and painful death*, he thought. *That would teach 'em.*

"Without the kindness of Zade's people, the land turned cold and barren. Hunger and illness plagued the people—and then it began to snow. Never before had any land known a snowfall like this one. It snowed and snowed and kept on snowing. In some places, the snow was thirty feet deep. The cold killed many o' the people.

"Those who survived began whisperin' of a mysterious

creature who prowled the land like a ghost, leavin' behind only giant pawprints as proof of its existence.

"The evil lord, whose powers were not enough to stop the snowstorm, finally retreated to the highest tower of his castle. Day and night he stood at the window and cursed the cold. He never left the tower room, and starin' out at the snow that had robbed him of his rule, he slowly lost his mind.

"One mornin', he spied a gigantic white cat pacing in the snow below, lookin' up at 'im with fire in its eyes. But when the evil lord sent word to have it killed, his men laughed. After all, he was a madman, and none of them had spied a giant cat in the snow.

"But the cat did indeed exist. It was a snow leopard— enormous, sleek, and muscular, with gray spots on its white coat and gold eyes set in an arrow-sharp face— and it stalked the castle fer many months, waitin' till the snow had risen so high that it could easily leap through the window o' the tower. But the snow leopard didn't kill the terrified tyrant. Instead, it simply looked 'im in the eyes—a long, fiery look. The evil lord recognized 'im at once: 'ZADE!' he cried in terror and instantly turned into a statue of granite.

"The snow leopard left the tower and ran fer the shore

where the prisoner ship had mysteriously returned and docked. No one knew if the prisoners were still on board, dead or alive, but they saw the snow leopard leap from the snowy bank onto the ship, which sailed away, never to be seen again. The lordless land remained covered in snow for four hundred years, and the few people who remained struggled to survive. Then fifty years ago, the ship *Mersades* appeared out of nowhere—with no captain, no crewmen, no passengers—but with a strong magic that melted the snow and revived the land and its people. Those who knew the old tale marveled when they saw the *Mersades'* masthead—a snow leopard! There seemed to be no doubt about it: this was the ship that had sailed away with Zade and his faithful followers, now come home to stay."

Everyone sat quietly at the end of Declan's story. Jayni's head was pounding with a dozen questions. She started with the most pressing one: "Was Zade a man before he was a snow leopard?"

"No one knows," answered Declan. "History speaks only of a mighty warrior without equal—a good and kind lord who insisted an even better lord was comin'. We don't know much more than that. But I do believe he existed."

"And he ruled *here*? In this land?"

Declan nodded.

"What is the name of this land anyway?" asked Jayni.

Declan's eyes looked out into the distance, as if he could see a hundred things no one else could.

"Ye are still in yer own land, dear one."

Jayni laughed. "This is *nothing* like my land. We don't have talking birds and magical ships and evil baby foxes!"

Declan chuckled, then chose his words carefully. "Sometimes . . . sometimes pain opens up a new world to us . . . an Everworld within our existing world. Pax's sufferin'—and yers too, as his friend—has opened yer eyes to what has been here all along."

Jayni paused before asking, "You mean, this world is still *my* world, but it's kind of a hidden part I've never noticed before?"

"Ye are quite an intelligent young lady," Declan praised her. "Ye said it better than I."

"But how does that work? How can I live in two worlds at once? And why does it feel like the longer I'm here, the more questions I have?

Declan beamed. "You're asking wise questions, lass. I admit, it's hard to understand—and even harder to explain. But it will make more sense soon."

Jayni opened her mouth to ask another question, but

Declan ended all conversation, saying, "We've rested long enough. There are many miles still to go—the most difficult miles."

Darya lifted Pax back into her arms. He let out a long raspy breath.

"He's still dangling in there!" declared Wilmer.

"Yes, he's hanging in there, Wilmer," Darya replied. Even after resting, she looked older to Jayni—frail even.

Suddenly, it dawned on Jayni that Darya was using every last bit of her magic to keep Pax alive.

8

White Willow

Now the narrow path ran steeply downhill, sometimes bumpy with rocks and sometimes slippery with loose dirt. Jayni's knees ached from all the pounding and slipping and sliding. But she couldn't stop thinking about Declan's story.

What happened after Zade left on that ship?

Did the people survive?

Did the Great Lord ever come like Zade promised?

Lost in her thoughts, Jayni didn't notice that the path was coming to an end, nor that the air felt heavy and gloomy. But she was jolted back to her senses when Wilmer came in for a crash landing, and Declan rolled like a potato all the way down the path and into a little gully. No one could hear exactly what he said, but it was obvious he was none too pleased.

And now Jayni saw the second most amazing sight in her travels.

Just beyond the gully was a glassy pond of dark water, as still and clear as a mirror. At the edge of the pond towered a magnificent white weeping willow tree, surrounded by thirty or forty smaller purple weeping willows. The white weeping willow stood like a tall bride, bedecked in her jewels and gown, all sparkling and dazzling and surrounded by her bridesmaids. Although there wasn't even the hint of a breeze, the tree moved and swayed and bent forward as if she were admiring herself in her liquid mirror.

Just as Jayni opened her mouth to gush over the willow's beauty, Pax's body shook with a violent chesty cough, and his eyes blinked open. Jayni whirled around and cried, "Pax!"

Darya, who was still cradling him tightly in her arms, blinked down at him with joy.

Pax tried to move his arms but couldn't. "What . . . what happened? Where am I?"

Jayni ran up to him and pressed her face close to his, nearly touching noses with him. "Pax! Pax, you're awake!

Oh, it's all my fault! You collapsed after the Bumfuzzles . . . after you rescued me—I was so selfish! And I've been *so* worried!"

"Me too!" declared Wilmer. "I've been one big worry pimple!"

Declan had recovered from his ugly fall, except for the dirt still in his beard. His face beamed as he said, "Good to see ye again, lad."

Darya set Pax down slowly as he began to regain movement in his legs and arms. Unwrapping him, she explained, "This swaddling put you into a deep sleep—a sleep that gave rest to your body and fought off infection."

"I got another infection?" asked Pax.

"Yes, it was awful." Jayni's eyes filled with tears. "You were burning up and gasping, just like last year when you ended up in the hospital. But Darya took care of you. She kept you alive."

Pax looked up at Darya and wished he could think of something better to say than just, "Thank you."

But Darya, obviously moved by those two little words, reassured him it was her joy to take care of him. "How do you feel now?" she asked.

Pax struggled to stand on his own. He took a couple wobbly steps.

"Weak . . . but okay."

"Oh! I have something for you!" Jayni reached into Pax's satchel, still slung across her chest, and pulled out the tiny flask of enchanted water. "Drink this!"

Pax took a sip and his eyes brightened. Then he drank till Jayni thought he might drown.

When he finally came up for air, he felt a little stronger—strong enough to take some more steps and look around. The last thing he'd seen was thick fog and wet grass and a hint of dawn—but now the sun felt hot and westerly, a sheer rocky mountainside loomed high beside him, and a pebbly dirt path sloped to the edge of a pond, at the far side of which grew the most stunning trees he'd ever seen. The mountain beside him appeared to converge with another mountain behind those trees.

"Where *are* we?" he asked.

"We're a day's journey from the cliffs where you so courageously rescued your friend," answered Declan. "And we're getting ready to take a narrow passageway between two mountains—a dangerous way, but the quickest way to the healing man."

Pax's eyes brightened. *The healing man.* In all the crisis and unconsciousness, he'd momentarily forgotten the reason that had compelled him to step into this world.

"We're headed for White Willow's Grove!" Wilmer blurted out.

"A grove?" Pax and Jayni asked at the same time.

Darya lowered her voice and looked at Pax. "Like Declan said, this is the fastest way to get you help, Lovie— passing between the mountains. Unfortunately, the passage is guarded by a wicked willow tree."

Pax raised his eyebrows and looked across the pond at the lofty and swaying willow. Jayni wondered how a tree could ever be *wicked*.

"The willow's even more dangerous than the Bumfuzzles," continued Darya. "We had planned to take another route, a safer route, but it would have taken several days more. When you collapsed, Pax, we realized how serious your condition is, and we knew this shortcut was our only option."

"There wasn't a moment to share!" piped in Wilmer. He glared at White Willow across the water, his bulging eyes set into a steely scowl, his feathered brow furrowed, and his wings pulled back as if he were ready to strike.

Darya continued, "White Willow is cruel. She preys on any negative emotion you feel—fear, anger, shame, worry—and she tortures you with it. She has crippled strong men with their own anger and beautiful women with their worry. Even her purple friends can cause great distress."

The children heard guttural sounds coming from Wilmer, as if he were growling at the willow now. Then he opened his beak wide with one of his bell calls.

"Wilmer, you're not helping," chided Declan.

The frazzled bird started pacing and muttering, "Colly-wobbles!" through his clenched beak.

"The only ones who have taken this way and survived are friends of the healing man," explained Darya. "But of course, you don't know him yet, so you are at great risk. However, if you do *exactly* as we say, Declan and I can get you safely to the other side, unharmed."

This time, Jayni resolved, *I'm going to listen closely and obey.*

"We'll walk through the grove in pairs," said Darya. "Pax, you with me. Jayni, you with Declan. White Willow will try to grasp you and entangle you in her branches—branches that transmit lies into your minds. You don't have to fight her branches . . . you just have to listen to our voices above hers. Don't stop listening to us, not even for a second. Do you understand?"

Jayni forgot to breathe. Pax twisted his hands together. But they both answered, "Yes."

Wilmer was to fly over the white and purple willows, through the narrow passageway, and wait for his friends on the other side.

The group was ready. Although Pax could now walk freely, he felt almost frozen with fear. If he could just make it to the other side to meet the healing man, it would all be worth it. With resolve, he took his first step forward.

Jayni was standing beside him and noticed the hope in his eyes. She stepped forward with him and reached out to give his hand a squeeze. Then she looked across the pond at White Willow. How sad that such a stunningly beautiful tree could in fact be wicked and threatening— a monster, not a bride.

Pax felt the air grow heavier and the light grow dimmer the closer they got to the willows, almost as if he were walking into the thickest blanket of fog, yet he could still see clearly.

The group slowly proceeded around the glassy pond till they were within arm's reach of the first menacing purple willow tree.

Jayni noticed there was no way around the willows. The two mountains were almost touching here, and the willows blocked all access to the narrow path that lay between them.

Pax took a deep breath. He watched as Declan and Jayni parted the branches, stepped forward, and disappeared into the trees. Then Darya pulled back the branches and said, "Follow closely, Lovie."

A healing man, he reminded himself. *A healing man.* Then he stepped behind Darya into the grove.

9

The Grove

Pax was instantly engulfed in willow branches, first purple, then white, hanging thick and low in every direction. The air was neither hot nor cold. It didn't feel like day or night, but something in between. Pax couldn't feel his feet on the ground, nor did he know if he'd taken two steps or two dozen before a voice started shrieking, "Life is pain! Pain that will never end! Your friends will have everything, and you will have nothing! Cancer is the end of it all! Give up! You're going to die!"

Pax threw his hands over his ears but then realized the voice was inside his head. These were thoughts that often came to him in the middle of sleepless nights, and now the wicked willow was torturing him with them.

"Everything good is being taken from you, and the

worst is yet to come! Death! Death!"

Pax's heart was pounding out of his chest, fear pulsed through his veins and throbbed in his head. He trembled from head to toe.

He saw Darya stop and turn around to face him. Her deeply compassionate spirit allowed her to feel what Pax felt. She looked into his eyes with her starry ones and said, "It makes sense that you're fearful, Pax. You've suffered so much. But you are loved, and I'm so happy to help you. This is not the end. Stay with me."

Pax felt Darya's courage and kindness wash over him. He realized she loved him and wasn't bothered by his panic, and she wasn't going to leave him. Instead, she was showing him a way through his terror.

"Keep following me, keep listening to me, Pax," Darya said as she turned back around to forge ahead through the unrelenting willow branches.

As he kept close behind Darya, Pax noticed the shrieking quieted to a holler, and then the holler faded to a whisper. Tears streamed down his cheeks. He had never told anyone but his parents how scared he was of dying. But Darya knew now, and it felt like someone had taken the heaviest backpack off his shoulders. He was no longer alone in his fear.

While Pax had been facing his worst nightmare, Jayni had been fighting overwhelming shame. She too was determined to follow and listen intently to Declan, but as the willow branches snatched at her, entangled her, a monster-like voice growled viciously in her ear, "You're not who everyone thinks you are. You're a fake, a fraud, a failure. No one knows who you *really* are, deep down . . . and if they did, they'd hate you. Leave you! Never be your friend!"

Jayni struggled to keep Declan in her sight. Endless branches laden with slender, pointy white leaves almost blinded her.

Whatever you do, don't take your eyes off Declan. Listen to him. You have to hear what he's saying, Jayni commanded herself.

The longer she repeated this to herself, the more she heard Declan's voice above the monstrous one: "They're lies, Jayni. Don't believe 'em. I know you feel shame, but ye are precious, ye are loved! Those hidden parts o' yer heart can be healed—if ye can just make it through t' the other side . . ."

Jayni wanted to believe him, but then, the lies felt so *true*. Maybe if Declan knew *everything* she'd done, the awful things she'd thought, how often she messed up—maybe then he would agree with the horrible monster.

The lies grew louder.

Jayni silently screamed at herself again—*Don't give in! Listen to Declan! Believe him!*

Declan briefly turned around and squared eyes with Jayni. "We're gonna make it, dear one. Stay with me. Keep listening to me."

Jayni nodded with a look that said, *I believe you even though these lies feel so real.*

The group was slowly making progress through the grove, pushing through the oppressive branches. Pax felt as if he were walking through liquid metal, and he was weary of fighting off the grasping, clawing, evil willow. He thought of Wilmer flying overhead, and wished with all his might he could soar right over the madness with him. Jayni wondered how big White Willow was. It seemed she went on forever.

Suddenly, a bright light slammed against their faces and they felt pushed out of the dark heavy air, out of the willows' cruel branches, out from between the two mountains. The children were gasping, sweating—and laughing. They dropped to their knees in utter exhaustion and looked at each other with astonishment and joy. Those hideous lies were gone. They'd made it!

Darya drew near the children, speaking words of encouragement and hugging them tight. "You children are so brave!"

Declan stepped away from the group, pulled out a big white handkerchief and wiped his eyes, then threw his scally-cap into the air with a belly laugh.

Wilmer had arrived before them and camped out on a rock, bulging eyes glued to the narrow willow-blocked opening between the mountains. Now he came flutter-hopping up to them, fluffing his feathers, wattles wagging wildly. "Well, I'll be! You just made it by the skin of your cheeks!"

10

The Mountain

On this side of the mountains stretched a vast sea, and above the sea glowed an orange-and-purple sunset. As Pax and Jayni flopped onto the sandy shore, they spotted the *Mersades*. The ship bobbed on the rippling water not far from the shoreline, her twinkle lights like fireflies in the sky and her hot cups of popple-cream no doubt ready to welcome the weary bunch.

Pax could have lingered for hours on this beautiful shore, but he'd feel safer once they boarded the vessel. With great effort, he struggled to stand up and start walking. Jayni followed.

Everyone slowly made their way across the sand to the ship's gangplank, which stretched all the way across the shallower water to the deck. Once there, they all nearly tumbled aboard—relieved over their victory against White Willow, but now speechless with exhaustion. They fell onto soft cushions and wrapped themselves in warm blankets, as Wilmer mumbled, "Hoist the sails . . . decks away."

The sails caught wind and pulled the ship farther away from the beach and into deeper waters.

Someone muttered, "We probably . . . should eat . . ."

But before the *Mersades* had moved another inch, everyone was fast asleep. Everyone except Jayni, that is. She fought against tired eyes as she looked around the ship, imagining Zade the snow leopard captaining the vessel and freeing his faithful followers who had been imprisoned below.

Then even Jayni drifted off to sleep, and the *Mersades* sailed into the darkening night.

Pax woke up coughing. Nights were always the worst.

He pulled himself up and out of the deep cushions of the deck's wraparound bench and reached for a cup of calming popple-cream. (*How did it always stay just perfectly* hot—*not enough to scald his tongue but just enough to soothe his throat?*) He sipped it as the boat rocked gently on the waves. Then he looked around at his sleeping friends, shadowy lumps of blankets dotting the bench.

What would it be like to sleep through the night without waking and coughing? he wondered.

His throat and chest soothed for the moment, he set the cup of popple-cream back onto the drink tray and rolled onto his back to sleep. But before he closed his eyes again, he gazed upward and his mouth dropped open.

The sky was an endless canopy of stars—millions of them. No, *billions* of them. Even though Pax had grown up in the mountains, where stars could be clearly seen away from the city lights, he had never seen such a massive sky, nor this many stars. He put his hands behind his head and stared into the expanse. He felt small. Very, very small. But somehow that comforted him.

Where are we? Pax wondered. *Is this another country . . . another world?*

He had no idea how long they'd been away from home, and his stomach knotted up every time he thought about how worried his parents might be—but not once had he thought to ask if this world had a name, or where it was located on a map (if it even appeared on one at all). Before getting sick two years ago, he'd been the smartest kid in his class—but now he forgot simple things, struggled for words, and felt like his head was full of fuzz.

Tomorrow I'll ask Declan, first thing, Pax resolved, then he drifted off to sleep once more.

But the morning brought new distractions, and Pax forgot about his question.

As the sun peeked over the horizon, the sleepers began to stir and stretch and rub their eyes.

From what Pax could tell, Darya had been up for hours already, tidying up and preparing breakfast. The smell of melted butter and maple syrup drew everyone like a magnet to the tea table she'd set up at the back of the boat.

Piled upon plates were stacks of pancakes dripping with maple syrup, bright red strawberries, and omelets cooked to perfection with everyone's favorite ingredients—"How did you know I like jalapeños?" cried Jayni—and crispy, hot strips of bacon glistening with deliciousness.

"Time to cow out!" cried Wilmer, as he buried his beak into a tall stack of pancakes.

"Wilmer, how do ye manage to get it wrong every single time? It's *pig* out, not *cow*," said Declan with a chuckle.

Wilmer looked up, syrup dripping from his wattles and a piece of bacon stuck to his beak.

Declan said through a mouthful of strawberries and pancake, "Life would be horribly dull without ye, me friend!"

As the friends feasted, they noticed in the distance a massive green mountain rising out of the water, its sky-high peak hidden in the clouds. As the ship drew nearer, an entire village could be seen built into the mountainside, with hundreds of small but colorful houses neatly stacked on top of each other. The uppermost houses had sunning decks while the sea-level houses had boating docks. In between the tightly packed houses were winding wooden staircases overgrown with fire lilies and jade vines. The effect was a spectacle of color and beauty.

But what fascinated Pax and Jayni most were the inhabitants of the village. As the *Mersades* sailed nearer to harbor, they couldn't take their eyes off the men and women and children of every age and giants and dwarfs and animals of every kind—for every one of them appeared to have either a disability or an illness.

They walked with white canes and gestured in sign language. Some shook uncontrollably, others were doubled over in pain. Some lay on stretchers, others used wheelchairs, and a few walked alongside their oxygen tanks.

Pax noticed they were all smiling or laughing.

"Who are they? Where are we?" asked Jayni.

"Welcome to Sage Mountain and the Village of Dree," Declan said with sparkling eyes and a flourish of his hand. There was something about the way he said it—like he was about to tell the best story in the world. But all he said was, "These are the happiest, helpingest, most hospitable creatures ye'll ever meet, fer they know the healin' man well. He lives at the top o' this mountain."

"*What!*" Pax was surprised at how loud his own voice sounded. "Then . . . why are they all . . . why is everyone so . . ."—he nodded toward the crowds since it was impolite to point—"if they've seen the *healing* man?"

Declan paused before answering. He glanced down at his wooden leg, then out toward the horizon, then back at Pax. "Lad, the healin' man is good through 'n' through. Ye have to believe that first, before the rest makes sense. *I* can't convince ye of his goodness—ye'll have to see for yerself."

Pax didn't say a word, but anger turned his insides hot. He was almost trembling with rage. Had he come all this way —endured danger and terror, spent what little energy he had—just to meet a healing man who didn't actually *heal*?

The *Mersades* swung hard to starboard, tied herself alongside the dock, and released her gangway. As Declan reached out to secure the bow line, he said, "We'll be warmly welcomed here and find comfortable lodging fer the night. Darya, would ye lead us to that first house off the docks—the one with the blue door?"

Darya, Wilmer, Declan, and Jayni made their way down the gangway and onto the floating dock, then up some wooden steps to a long pier that led to a maze of docks connected to the sea-level houses. But Pax lagged behind, sullen and brooding.

Jayni looked back at him, then turned away quickly and ran to join Darya in front. Sometimes she didn't understand Pax. Sometimes she felt as if he pushed her away. Most of the time she didn't know what to do or say. She hated that cancer had changed Pax, not just on the outside but on the inside as well. Cancer had robbed her of her energetic, fun-loving, free-spirited best friend. She felt anger welling up inside her.

Declan slowed his hobbling steps till Pax caught up with him. The two walked along in silence. Ahead of them, the rest had reached the first little house. Darya knocked on the blue door, and an old woman welcomed them in.

Declan halted and turned to face Pax. Almost in a whisper he said, "Lad, I'm so sorry for what ye've had to suffer. My heart breaks to think of a child enduring the cruelty o' cancer."

Pax remained rigid, eyes staring straight ahead, hands clenched into fists at his side. He doubted that Declan or any of the others, even Jayni, could imagine how desperately he wanted to be healed. He'd probably give anything to be like he was before—when he could eat pizza without getting sick to his stomach, play soccer as well as the other boys, and go to school every day, no matter how much he didn't like getting up at six o'clock in the morning.

Declan continued, as if choosing his words carefully. "I was not quite as young as ye—nor nearly as sick—but I'll ne'er forget starin' death in the face at the tender age o' twelve." He paused. "Doctors took this leg to save me life."

Pax turned, looking into Declan's face.

"I was in the hospital fer weeks. And then when I did return home, I couldn't run around with me friends anymore. Couldn't hike hills or explore caves. Had to learn to walk all o'er again, this time with a wooden beast o' a leg. I was sad, angry, lonely. It felt like no one could understand."

Pax blinked back tears. Declan adjusted his scally-cap and stroked his long beard. They stood there together while the sun ducked behind thick layers of coastal fog. The air was cool and salty.

Pax was afraid to speak. He knew his voice might crack

with emotion, or worse yet, he might burst into tears. But he slowly worked up the courage to ask, "Then how did you . . . I mean, you're so kind and patient. How did you . . ."

"Deal with all the sadness and anger?" Declan gently finished for him.

Pax nodded.

Declan took a step forward and motioned for Pax to walk with him. They made their way up the dock and toward the shore.

"Well, I *didn't* fer a good year or two. I was angry at everyone round me who was livin' a normal life with two good legs. That's when I packed me bags and headed south. Ended up at the Bay of Bumfuzzles and quickly fell prey to the monsters' flattery. But the healin' man rescued me. Changed me."

"But he didn't actually *heal* you," Pax said bitterly.

"He didn't heal me leg, no. But I finally understood why I was special . . . and why I was left hobblin'," said Declan.

"Why?" asked Pax, his tone desperate.

Declan and Pax had stepped off the dock onto a paved path that passed by a bustling marketplace to their right. Before Declan could answer Pax, a little boy rushed up to him and threw his arms around him, crying, "I missed you!" This caught the attention of several other people and animals who quickly made their way over to Declan as well. Pax watched as Declan embraced a skunk with a scarred face, a young lady with a guide dog, an elderly man who used an oxygen tank, and a limping lop-eared rabbit. When Declan introduced him, Pax smiled with surprise at their enthusiastic welcome and unreserved hugs. His clenched hands relaxed, his face softened, and his pent-up breath released into a long sigh. He instantly felt like he belonged here, with these people and creatures. He wanted to stay and talk with them, but Declan was explaining, "Pax and I are headed to Miss Cassidy's house, but we'll rejoin you as soon as we can."

As the two walked up the path toward the tiered houses, Declan returned to Pax's question. "The healing man left me a wee bit broken so I could understand"—he looked back at his friends—"Kai and Tilly, Roe, Reece, and Jed. And dozens o' others. When a sufferin' creature shows up at me cottage, I get to help 'em and bring 'em here. Show 'em the way up the mountain. Fact is, they probably wouldn't listen to me if I didn't have this wooden stump. It's proof that I've suffered too."

"Why do you bring them here? Why do they all live together here?"

Declan took a deep breath and adjusted the scally-cap on his head. "Well, that is quite the mystery. While ye were sleeping in Darya's arms earlier, I explained to Jayni that pain invites us into a world within our existing world. Did ye realize ye never even left yer own world when ye came here? Ye simply entered the Everworld—a hidden dimension ye were blind to before. The folk of Dree still live in their own respective worlds, with lots of pain and sadness—but they live here as well, knowin' happiness and friendship that helps 'em get through the sufferin' better. These sufferin' ones know a secret so good it would make yer head spin. It changes everythin'. That's why ye need to get to the top o' the mountain and meet *him*."

Declan's eyes grew soft as he added, "And sooner or later, lad—he *does* heal everyone physically. Sometimes he heals them right away, just as soon as they arrive here. And sometimes he waits till . . . well, till much later."

11

The Village of Dree

Jayni bristled when Pax and Declan entered through the blue door of Miss Cassidy's house. She noticed the transformation in Pax—he was smiling, relaxed . . . *different.* And for reasons she could not explain, it annoyed her.

"Come on in, shweetpeash, and join the feshtiviteesh!" shouted a rickety old woman with a hunched back and quite a few missing teeth. *This must be Miss Cassidy,* thought Pax.

"I'm happy to have y'all here, jusht make yourshelf at home. Tea'sh on the shtovetop, jam and bread'sh in the pantry."

With the help of a wooden cane, she shuffled over to a well-worn chair, bent forward, bones creaking, and sank into it. Immediately she fell asleep.

There was a knock on the front door, but before anyone had a chance to answer it, the door swung open and in came a furless fox, a wingless fairy, and a young girl in a wheelchair.

The fairy ran straight for Declan.

"Oh, Declan!" she said in a tiny tinkling voice, "I love it here! I do! I finally met the healing man, and now I—"

But her voice was drowned out by Miss Cassidy who woke with a jolt and shouted,

"Good, good! Come on in! Ish everyone elsh on their way?" then promptly fell back asleep before anyone could answer her question.

Everyone else? thought Jayni. The small house was already feeling snug—but sure enough, a huge gray ogre squeezed through the door, followed by a boy with a cleft palate, and then an ocelot named Odin, who'd been born with only one eye.

Darya floated around the tiny kitchen, filling teacups with steaming peppermint tea and chipped blue plates with buttered toast. The house hummed with introductions and reunions and laughter.

Pax was usually shy in a group of new people, but he chatted easily with the girl who used a wheelchair. Jayni sipped tea with the ocelot (and sneaked curious little peeks at Pax across the room from her). Wilmer fluttered here and there, making sure everyone heard about his near-death experiences with the Bumfuzzles.

After an hour of lively conversation, and five more creatures had joined them—for a grand total of twenty squeezed into a house no bigger than Pax's living room back home—Declan cleared his throat and said in a loud voice, "Welcome, everyone! May I have yer attention? I have an announcement t'make."

The room fell silent, except for the soft *tinking* of dishware. Everyone looked eagerly at Declan.

Jayni sneaked one last peek at Pax. He looked so happy, so relaxed. He didn't seem out of place here. From the moment he'd stepped into the house, he'd been confident and chatty. It made her feel unsettled—jealous even. *Why was Pax happier with perfect strangers than he'd been with her, his best friend, these past couple of years?*

When Declan stood up, he was still shorter than most of those who were sitting, but his presence commanded attention. All eyes were on him. "We have new friends with us," Declan beamed. "I think most o' ye have already had a chance to meet 'em. Tomorrow they will make their way up the mountain to find the healin' man."

A spontaneous and almost deafening cheer erupted

in the crowded room. The fairy cried happy tears, and the ogre let out a loud but glad grunt, and Miss Cassidy, who had managed to keep herself awake for Declan's announcement, thumped her cane on the floor with joy.

But one person in the room was silent.

Jayni stood in the corner, her unsettled feeling growing into frustration. I *don't need the healing man*, she silently argued. *I'm not sick or disabled.*

She felt a brief pang of guilt. *Remember how you fell for the Bumfuzzles?*

But Jayni quickly dismissed the thought. *How did this adventure become all about Pax? He can go up the mountain by himself. I'm not going.*

Declan was still talking.

"Now, ye all know what a formidable trek this is, and how much courage it takes to make it to the top. I thought we might send these two off right with a Dree Gala at the foot o' the mountain tonight." Another great cheer went up, then everyone started talking at once, and Pax and Jayni caught only fragments of the excited chatter:

". . . to pitch the tent!"

". . . and when the fire is kindled . . ."

"I'll bring the apple skewers . . ."

Jayni momentarily forgot about her inner turmoil as

she listened to the excitement. She had no idea what a Dree Gala was, but if all the hubbub was any clue, it must be wonderful.

Pax was already smitten with everything and everyone in Dree, so Declan could have suggested they clean someone's messy bedroom, and he would have been thrilled. But Pax was also tired—*exhausted.* His head throbbed. His legs and feet felt heavy and immovable, as if they'd been filled with wet cement.

A sea-goat, who had been the last to squeeze into the house, noticed Pax's pale face and offered to let him nap in his quiet home.

"Or-or you c-c-could nap on the dock in the sun-un if you-you pre-pre-prefer," said the kind creature who introduced himself as Guddle. He experienced constant tiny seizures that made his body tremble and caused him to stutter his words.

Pax smiled gratefully, said his goodbyes to his friends old and new, and followed Guddle to the seventh house down the lane—green with white shutters, tidy and quiet. It was as simply furnished as the old woman's, and it gave off that same spirit of welcome and belonging. He instantly felt at home and curled up on a soft green couch in the corner under a large window that let the sun in.

Warm and cozy, he was asleep within minutes.

Pax dreamed he was flying over a dark sea toward a black mountain half-covered in clouds. And at the top of the mountain was a man made of lava—his body glowed with fire, and his eyes were shooting flames. Pax was terrified of the lava man, but he couldn't stop himself from flying nearer and nearer. Then he realized he had a head full of curly black hair again, and his arms were strong and muscular, and he wasn't coughing. He tried to stop flying, but still he sped faster and faster toward the lava man . . .

Pax was startled out of his dream by the sound of a loud drum—*ba-rum-pum-pum-BONG! Ba-rum-pum-pum-BONG!* He pulled himself up to look out the window and was shocked to see the sun setting over the water. How long had he slept? He walked across the room and opened the front door. To his left, down by the pier, a huge crowd had gathered—perhaps all of Dree—carrying colorful banners and baskets of food and torches and driving carts piled high with chairs and blankets and firewood. Now, along with the drumming, he could hear laughing and singing.

Suddenly he remembered how much he disliked big crowds. The noise and energy exhausted him. But he loved the citizens of Dree and resolved to join them, no matter how overwhelming it might be. He walked down the row of houses and up to the throng of merrymakers, where he found a place to stand between a miniature white unicorn and a baby red panda.

He caught a glimpse of Jayni on the far side of the crowd—she was giggling and throwing confetti with a pixie. Darya hovered above the crowd, holding a large garland of flowers. She saw Pax and smiled and waved. She cupped her hand to her mouth and yelled down into the crowd, "He's here, Declan!"

Pax tried to follow her gaze but couldn't see the little Hobblechaun from where he stood.

The drum stopped beating, and a loud, obnoxious bell blasted.

Well, Wilmer's definitely here, Pax thought, chuckling to himself.

The crowd quieted just enough to hear Declan shout, "Let the Dree Gala begin!"

And then a deafening roar went up, and the drum beat louder than ever, and white-and-silver fireworks burst into falling stars overhead. The crowd began moving as one big body away from the village and toward the far side of the mountain, just as the sun turned out its light.

The tallest creatures held up torches and lanterns to

light the way, and the shouting and cheering became
a song:

Light the dark way, dear!
Hold your head high!
Dark is the world
But hope's on our side!

Sing for the weary
Wait for the weak
Laugh, ye are broken—
Broken but FREE!

Tralla la! Chirry-aye!
Biddy-um, bum-bum!
Tralla la! Chirry-aye!
Biddy-um, bum-bum-bum!

The festive crowd slowed to a stop when they reached
a wide sandy beach at the eastern side of the mountain.
About twenty creatures immediately went to work pitch-
ing a tent—a white, five-sided tent as big as a house.
Darya gently draped the garland of flowers around its top.
Lanterns were hung inside, and tall serving tables were
unfolded to hold baskets brimming with food.

Outside, torches were set into stakes stuck in the sand,

and blankets were unrolled. A family of dwarfs built two bonfires, and a skinny giant helped those with walkers and wheelchairs out of the sand and onto a broad wooden platform built beside the tent.

Despite their physical disabilities and limitations, each person and animal had a job to do, a skill to contribute. Even a man with no arms and no legs used his teeth to tighten ropes around the tent.

Pax had felt so useless for the past two years that he looked on with longing. Did *he* have anything to contribute to this gala? His thoughts were interrupted when Jayni ran by him into a circle of creatures dancing a jackdaw jig—a clapping, kicking, swirling group dance. After the dancing there was apple-roasting, and after apple-roasting came a rowdy game of snollygosters (Pax later said it was like playing charades and duck-duck-goose at the same time). And after that, there were hours more of dancing and singing and eating and playing and laughing. And whenever anyone grew tired, they napped on a blanket in the sand till they were strong enough to rejoin the fun.

It must have been long past midnight now, and those who were still awake sat around one of the bonfires telling stories—stories of heroes and conquests, ancient stories of Dree, but mostly stories of *him*, the healing man.

Pax had been curled up on a quilt just outside the bonfire circle, dozing off and on, but at the first mention of the healing man, he'd sat up slowly and listened in. He wanted to know every last detail about this mysterious man who didn't seem to actually heal anyone. But even though these creatures hadn't been cured of their illnesses and injuries, they earnestly loved the healing man, and Pax found himself longing to meet him more than ever before.

As Pax listened, he looked at the people and animals gathered around the fire and realized that Declan, Wilmer, Darya, and Jayni were all there, joining in the laughter and storytelling. It felt so comforting to be here in this place with his friends. Pax smiled when Jayni turned to look at him, but she didn't smile back. In fact, she hadn't spoken to him since they'd chatted over pancakes and bacon on the *Mersades* early that morning. Was she mad at him? It sure seemed like it. But why? The more he thought about it, the more he was convinced she *was* upset, and that made him upset in return, especially considering what she'd put him through with the Bumfuzzles. *How dare you be mad at* me *when* you're *the one who messed everything up?*

Thankfully, Wilmer kept commenting on everyone's

stories, misusing words like "chipper," and "cranky," till Pax was laughing so hard, he momentarily forgot about Jayni.

Soon, the power of full stomachs and good stories and a warm fire took its effect, and one by one they all fell asleep in an uneven circle around the glowing embers. The last thing Pax remembered was Wilmer chanting,

"Goodnight,

sleep upright,

don't let the bed bugs fight."

12

The Argument

Declan gently shook Pax awake, whispering, "Today's the day, lad. Time to go up the mountain."

Pax's eyes shot open, wide with expectation. He watched Declan gingerly step over a snoring Wilmer and pat Jayni on the shoulder.

"Wake up, dear one. Today's the day."

After only four hours of sleep, Pax should have been too exhausted to budge. But this morning his heart leaped and his mind raced, fueling his frail body. He wasn't sure what to expect, but with all his heart he wanted to meet the healing man.

Jayni, on the other hand, woke up grumpy. She dreaded the thought of hiking up the mountain with Pax. She'd seen a change in him here, and she wasn't sure how to interact with him now, nor could she make sense of all the feelings inside of her. *Of course* she wanted Pax to meet the healing man, but she also wanted . . . well, she wasn't sure what she wanted. She'd rather ignore everything going on in her heart and head. She rolled over and groaned. But Declan stood there looking down at her, waiting patiently—so she slowly forced herself up into a sitting position, then she stood, stretched, and pushed out a "Good morning."

There was just enough light in the sky for the three of them to see their way around all the sleeping bodies. Carefully they tiptoed to the large tent where they grazed through the baskets full of food. Declan instructed them to pack enough food for a whole day, so they filled Pax's satchel with boysenberries and sandwiches, carrot sticks and guacamole, roasted almonds and dark chocolate truffles. Then they filled two flasks full of still-hot popple-cream.

Although Jayni didn't want to go on this trek, the sight of such scrumptious food did help lighten her spirits for a moment. Then Declan announced something that made her spirits droop again.

"Dear ones, ye must climb the mountain without me. I cannuh go with ye for this part of the journey." Declan stuffed a couple extra snacks into Pax's satchel as he spoke.

"*Why* can't you go with us?" Pax asked, frowning. He was already nervous about climbing the mountain with an irritable friend, but now he was alarmed at the thought of going without a wise guide.

"Lad, no one is allowed up unless the healing man invites them. And once ye've gone up, ye cannot go again till . . ." He paused and thoughtfully stroked his long white beard. "Ye'll understand soon enough."

Jayni sat down on a chair in the food tent and put her elbows to her knees, chin in her hands.

Pax glanced sideways at her, then back at Declan. "How long will we be up there?"

"That's hard t' say. As I'm sure you've noticed, time works a wee bit differently here in the Everworld. It's not faster nor slower than yer time, but it's the kind o' time that doesn't fit on clocks or calendars." Declan lowered his voice and leaned forward, as if he were about to share a well-guarded secret. "It's called Extraordinary Time—moments filled with such special meaning that time is almost suspended."

Pax smiled and nodded slowly. Declan was perfectly describing how he'd been feeling since he'd entered this mysterious realm. It reminded him of the summer he went to science camp—the excitement of a new adventure, spending seven days in a cabin with new friends, experiencing new activities and routines. He'd been changed by that week—which hadn't really felt like a week at all, but rather a second and a month all at the same time.

Then a shadow fell across his face. "When we get back home, will it be the same time we left? I keep wondering if our parents are worrying about us."

At this, both Pax and Jayni desperately wanted to look at each other. They'd both wondered the same thing, yet they still refused to make eye contact. Instead, they glued their gaze on Declan.

Declan handed Pax his satchel, now bulging with snacks. "Just the perfect amount of time will have passed when ye return—no more, no less." And with that, Declan snapped back into action, saying, "Come along then. It's time ye were off."

Jayni sighed and forced herself up onto her feet, and Pax slung his satchel across his chest as Declan led them out of the tent and toward the foot of the mountain. The ground sloped upward and turned damp and mossy, then a few steps later they were climbing the hill with oaks and pines and firs.

A small wooden sign with the words "*In mundo patiens—Spero!*" marked the beginning of a path. Pax started to ask what the sign meant, but Jayni interrupted, "Do I *have* to go?"

The question punched Pax in the gut. Jayni knew what climbing this mountain meant to him. Plus, she was the one who'd been excited about going on an adventure. Why would she leave him now?

But Declan didn't look at all surprised. He smiled knowingly and reached up to pat her arm. "No one is forcin' ye to go, dear one. But know this: if ye decide *not* to go, ye'll deeply regret it."

Without giving her a chance to reply, Declan turned to Pax and said, "One final word of instruction, lad: *No matter what*, ye must keep to the path. It is narrow and sometimes quite difficult, and ye will be tempted to take short-cuts, but they will lead ye away from the healin' man. Stay on the path—it is well marked and will take ye safely to the top."

With that, Declan smiled at both children, then quickly turned and hobbled back to join the others who were now stirring from their sleep.

Pax half-looked at Jayni as he asked, "Well, are you going or staying?"

"I don't know," Jayni said coldly. "Do you even *want* me to go? Maybe you wanna take one of your *new* friends, since you seem to be so happy when you're with *them*."

Pax felt his chest tighten. He and Jayni rarely argued, but suddenly she was accusing him of—*what*? Making new friends? Was she jealous?

"Really?" he fired back. "Are you serious?" His pale face flushed with anger. "Of course, you wouldn't understand. Your life is *perfect*."

His voice grew louder with every word. "You've had, what?—a few colds and flus in your whole life. I can't remember what it feels like to be healthy for *one day*, Jayni! You get to eat anything you want . . . you go to school and play soccer and do all the normal kid stuff without wondering if it's going to *kill* you!"

Pax was on full blast now. He took a quick breath before almost yelling, "And when I *finally* get the chance to maybe be healed, you go and mess everything up and fall for some ridiculous Bumfuzzles' trick, and then you don't want me making new friends—and you sulk about hiking a mountain with me! I—I thought you were my best friend, Jayni—not my—*enemy*!"

Jayni had never seen Pax mad, had never heard him express such strong feelings. She stood there dumbstruck, at first feeling more shocked than wounded. She didn't know what to say and couldn't find any words.

This surprised Pax in return. He'd expected her to argue, rally a defense—but he wasn't prepared for silence.

He'd never acted like that, toward anyone, and suddenly he wanted to take back everything he'd said. He felt sick to his stomach. Where did this meanness come from? He *knew* that Jayni's life wasn't perfect. He knew he couldn't ask for a better friend. And now, as he stood there looking at Jayni's kind face with those almond-shaped eyes that usually glimmered with excitement—he was really seeing her for the first time in a long time—it dawned on him how hard these past two years must have been for her too. He had only ever thought about his own suffering, not hers. He trembled as the full weight of it all hit him.

"Jayni. I'm . . . I'm so . . . *sorry.*" His voice cracked. He blinked back tears.

Still Jayni didn't say a word.

"Those were terrible things to say," Pax stuttered. "I . . . I . . . don't know what I was thinking. It was so wrong of me. So awful."

He was relieved when he began coughing because it broke up the awkward, heavy silence. Over the years he'd often wished Jayni wouldn't talk so much. Now he desperately wanted her to say something. Anything.

Instead, Jayni began to cry. Little tears at first. And then great big sobs. Her shoulders shook, her nose turned red, and her eyes puffed up. She shuddered as she drew a deep breath. Finally, she choked out, "Oh, Pax, it's just horrible, isn't it? Sickness and selfishness. They just mess everything up."

Pax's eyes got watery again. "Yeah."

They both wiped their eyes and noses and looked at each other with fresh appreciation.

"Jayni?"

"Yeah?"

"You're my . . . best friend."

"You're mine too, Pax."

"I know this cancer has hurt you too," he said. "I'm sorry."

Jayni looked at Pax for a second, then threw her arms around him and cried into his T-shirt.

Pax and Jayni hadn't hugged each other since they were toddlers—not even after their biggest fight in the Climbing Tree that summer when they were seven. But Pax was glad for the hug, and he returned it with a full heart.

Jayni stepped back and sniffled. "I think I probably need to meet the healing man as much as you do. Can I go with you?"

Pax smiled. "I couldn't make it without you."

13

The Dragon Snake

They were running behind now, which meant they might not reach the summit before sunset. But the act of forgiving each other had energized them, and they set out at a quick pace, hiking uphill in quiet gratitude for one another. The air was cool and crisp, and the path was narrow but easy to follow, just as Declan had said. The orangish-brown dirt beneath their feet felt silty and loose, the trees lining the path on either side grew thick and tall, and the birds flitted between branches, singing.

The two walked in silence for a while, deep in thought. These last days (or at least what *felt* like days in this place where no clocks or calendars were used) had been the craziest, most magical, most unexpected of their lives. But somehow they both knew that the greatest experience was still to come—it was waiting for them at the top of this mountain.

"Do you think he'll heal you, Pax?" Jayni finally asked as she ducked under a low-hanging tree branch.

Pax took a few steps before answering, "I don't know." And then in an even softer voice he said, "I hope so."

The path grew narrow and knobby with giant tree roots. Prickly pine branches snagged their shirts and poked at their faces till the two could no longer walk side by side. Pax stepped back to let Jayni lead the way.

"No, Pax. You go first. I trust you."

Pax's heart swelled. It had been so long since he'd taken the lead in anything. His frail body had forced him to submit to countless pains and procedures, to quietly sit on the sidelines watching those who were healthy and energetic do all the things he couldn't do. Jayni's vote of confidence gave him courage, and he walked a little taller as he forged ahead.

But his courage didn't last long. A movement and a flash of color came from high up in the tree branches to his right. He stopped abruptly. The hairs of his arm stood on end.

Jayni came to a halt just behind him. "What was that?" she whispered.

Pax didn't answer, didn't move a muscle—he just

stared up into the thick curtain of pine needles.

"Don't be ssscared," hissed a voice that sounded compassionate and cruel at the same time. "I'm on your ssside."

Jayni grabbed Pax's arm. Pax was just as terrified as she was, but he had never seen Jayni show fear like this. He wouldn't have admitted it, but he enjoyed feeling like the strong one, like he was needed. He gathered up his courage and commanded, "Come out and show yourself, whoever you are!"

"Cccertainly," it hissed.

Now the branches above their heads shifted violently and there came a sound like sand being poured into a bucket. Bright colors flashed, and Pax and Jayni looked up to see a terrifying sight—a massive, slithering dragon-like snake. The body shimmered with orange and green scales which stood on end along the center of its back and ran the length of its forked tail. It wound itself around and strained the thinner branches of the trees as it descended. Two feathered wings stuck out from the sides of the body, giving it—Pax realized with horror—the power to wreak havoc from below *and* above where it now hung over them. The unblinking, iridescent eyes of its dragon head shone like green glass and focused on both children. The creature reminded Pax of the spiny bush viper he'd admired at the zoo last year—but this was an enormous and dreadful version.

The dragon snake smiled, revealing a hideous mouth with two fangs that grew out of its upper jaw, curved downward toward the lower jaw, and ended in sharp points. A red ribbon-like tongue unfurled between them as it spoke. "No need to be ssscared. I'm only here to *help.*"

The dragon snake coiled itself around a large branch, then lowered its head so that it was face-to-face with Pax and Jayni. It narrowed its shimmering green eyes and whispered, "Have you been told that sssilly old myth about a healing man living at the top of thisss mountain?"

Pax trembled, and Jayni grabbed onto his arm more tightly.

"I can sssee by your eyesss that you have," said the creature. Then shaking its head slowly, hissed, "Sssuch a pity. Giving falssse hope to the sssuffering. That sssad tale hasss been told for yearsss, and hundredsss of pitiful creaturesss have sssummited thisss mountain, only to find a weak old man and have all their dreamsss dashed."

Pax and Jayni froze as the dragon snake moved in closer.

Its body was still coiled around the branches above. "I know a better placccce where you can—"

Then, out of nowhere, right in the middle of the snake's

silky words, Pax heard a voice whisper into his ear . . .

"Use the seed."

Pax glanced sideways at Jayni, then looked back at the dragon snake to see if they had heard the voice too. But neither one gave any indication they had.

With his eyes still fixed on the dragon snake, Pax stealthily slipped his hand into the satchel. He felt around—there was the food they'd packed, the black concealing cloth, one last chewing leaf, and . . . *the seed!* It was the shape and size of an almond, and he grabbed it tightly and oh . . . so . . . slowly . . . pulled . . . it . . . out.

Now what? he thought.

The snake was still hissing on, ". . . and he'sss a crazy old loon who doesn't care a sssnit for anyone, but they keep sssending poor ssssouls up here to . . ."

But Pax couldn't hear the dragon snake because more words were being whispered into his ear (or was it coming from inside his head?), as clearly as if Jayni herself were speaking.

"Plant the seed."

Plant it? But how? Pax glanced down at the trampled dirt path. Without a shovel or tool of some sort, it would be almost impossible to get the large seed into this hard-as-a-rock ground.

The dragon snake now turned his attention to Jayni, steadily inching closer to her.

The longer she stared at it the more and more familiar the face became. And although she wanted to run or scream, she knew Pax was working out a plan. From the corner of her eye, she'd seen his hand moving through his satchel. So, she held steady, waiting for Pax to act.

"Sssuch a pretty girl, you are. And obviously sssmart. Why don't you come with me, and I'll show you . . ."

Pax's rattling lungs exploded into a deep chesty cough—and that gave him an idea. He kept his eyes on the snake, pretending to listen intently to it, then forced himself into another bout of violent coughing. He doubled over, quickly dropping the seed to the ground and covering it with the heel of his right foot. He gave a few more good coughs, then stood upright again.

The snake cast a sideways glance at Pax, but Jayni held her gaze steady, and the snake continued its creepy monologue.

Pax shifted all his weight onto his right foot. With as little movement as possible, he rotated his heel left, then right, then left again—trying to screw the seed into the ground.

But now the dragon snake was growing suspicious.

It noticed Pax's awkward movements and the distracted look in his eyes—and with one swift movement, it uncoiled its body from the branch above, dropped to the ground, and sprang toward Pax's feet.

Pax jumped toward Jayni, sending them both sprawling to the ground.

The snake landed like a gigantic rubber hose just beyond the seed.

At that moment, the seed shot a giant vine straight out of the ground. Solid and shiny as metal and its branches and leaves razor sharp, it sliced through the air, growing up and out till it formed a formidable barrier between the children and the dragon snake.

Pax gasped. In the center of the vine hung a long, silver dagger. Without hesitating, Pax yanked it off, handed it to Jayni, then yelled at the dragon snake on the other side of the vine, "Now you're in trouble!"

Jayni had always won the swordfights when they'd fought pretend battles. It didn't matter what the "swords" actually were—wooden spoons, old curtain rods, sticks from the forest—she had swiftly beaten Pax every time. He had no doubt that even now, faced with a hideous creature and an untested dagger, Spitfire would come out the victor—as always.

The dragon snake was enraged. It swiftly coiled its body, leaped diagonally into the tree branches overhead, then back down to the other side of the metal vine, within striking distance of the children. It recoiled its body, arched its neck, and stretched its feathered wings wide.

In the time it had taken the snake to do this, Pax and Jayni had rushed off the opposite edge of the path, then whirled around to see the snake lying opposite them in perfect position to strike. With the foot-long dagger in her right hand, Jayni took one step toward the vile reptile and pointed the knife toward its face, which was now turning red. Smoke began seeping from the nostrils.

Jayni panicked. *Can it breathe fire?* she wondered, as her dagger hand began to shake.

Pax saw the smoke rising and frantically tried to think of a way to help. He shoved his hand back into the satchel and yanked out the black concealing cloth. With one swift motion, he stepped forward and threw it onto Jayni's head. It instantly grew to cover her, right down to her toes, and she disappeared from sight. Pax knew she could still see them perfectly well, but the dragon snake could no longer see her.

The snake's shock and confusion gave Pax enough time to leap right and duck behind a tree.

All was quiet. The kind of quiet that makes seconds feel like hours. The dragon was still coiled, whipping its head around in all directions in search of its prey. The nostrils smoked, and the green eyes flashed. It reared back as if drawing a great breath, then shot its head forward again and blew a stream of fire from its mouth toward the spot where the children had once stood.

Pax could feel its heat even from behind the tree. He didn't know where Jayni was now, but he knew he had to act fast. He jumped behind the metal vine opposite the snake and silently crept alongside it till he could peek around it to see the dragon snake's forked tail. Now if he could just grab the tail and cause a distraction, maybe Jayni would have a chance to strike.

But before he made his next move, the dragon snake flung back its head, roaring in pain. At the same time, Jayni threw off the concealing cloth, revealing not only herself but also a bloodied dagger.

Now the dragon snake writhed and twisted, and with the last ounce of its life, it used both fire and fangs to strike wildly at the children on both sides of the path.

But Pax and Jayni saw that the creature was fatally wounded, unable to slither or pounce, so they ran up the path a safe distance where they huddled together, trembling, till the dragon snake dropped to the ground in a smoky, scaly heap.

Neither child said anything for a long time. When Jayni realized she was still holding the bloodied dagger in her trembling hand, she threw it into a thick clump of trees along the path. Her hands were stained with dragon snake blood, which made her shiver.

Pax had noticed the blood too and had already reached inside his satchel for the tiny flask of enchanted water. He handed it to Jayni, who gratefully took it and began washing her hands.

"Pax. I saw its face when I stabbed it. It looked like the Bumfuzzles—you know, that evil, grotesque face they got after they transformed? And its voice . . . Didn't it sound exactly like White Willow? I think something evil is after us," Jayni said, shuddering.

Pax nodded, then without a word, he slumped to the ground. His muscles cramped, his head ached, and his chest heaved. "I need . . . to rest. Just for a few minutes," he whispered.

It was then that Jayni noticed how pale he looked and how bony and sickly he was. This long quest had taken every bit of the little energy Pax had left—but he had never complained.

"Pax. I think you're too sick to keep going."

He took a deep breath and forced words out of his mouth. "I know how to . . . push through. We're almost there anyway. I . . . just need to . . . catch my breath."

Jayni felt her insides twist up. She was angry that the path to healing was only making things worse.

"Why did Declan say the path would take us safely to the top? That wasn't safe at all. That was awful!" cried Jayni.

Pax was hunched over, holding his head in his hands. But he said weakly, "But we had everything we needed. Actually, we've . . . had it all along. And the snake . . . didn't win in the end. We *are* safe."

Jayni was quiet.

"Maybe safe doesn't mean *easy*," added Pax with great effort. "Maybe it means we get there all right, but there's still gonna be danger . . . all along the way." Pax struggled for his next breath.

"I hate it when you're right," said Jayni with a little smile. Then the smile vanished. "It's just that I really want you to be healed and strong and to come back to school and play sports and . . ." Her voice trailed off.

"I do too, Spitfire. I do too." Then Pax, unable to say or do anything else, laid his head down on the dirt path and fell asleep.

Jayni stood watching her friend, so pale and still he almost seemed lifeless. She'd never felt pain like this. It wasn't physical pain, but it still hurt every inch of her body. It was the pain of watching one of her favorite people in the world slowly grow sicker and weaker. It was the grief of wondering if he would die. It was the longing for life to be different, to be better, to be like other people's normal lives. Why was this happening to them? What was the point of all this pain?

14

The Snowstorm

It felt afternoonish when the two finally resumed their uphill hike. They'd lost time arguing back at the bottom of the hill, fighting the dragon snake, and resting after the fight, so they weren't even halfway up the mountain. Both silently wondered if they would have to spend the night in the woods. They ate as they walked—a handful of almonds, a chocolate truffle, boysenberries, sandwiches. After eating, Pax and Jayni took turns drinking from the magical flask and were revived by its water.

Up ahead stood a weathered wooden sign staked into the ground with an arrow pointing right: ICE CREAM SHOPPE AND RIDE TO THE TOP. TURN HERE.

"Ice cream! Up here?" asked Pax.

"It's obviously a trap," said Jayni with a voice of authority.

"To get us off the path."

Pax smiled at her. "Good point. But maybe there really *is* an ice cream shop. Wouldn't that be weird?"

"Well, I don't want to find out," Jayni said, passing the sign without even a sideways glance. "I've gotten into enough trouble for . . . well, however long it's been in Extraordinary Time," Jayni finished with a laugh.

Pax laughed with her and the two continued their trek uphill, happy that they'd resisted temptation (while also the slightest bit curious about whether the ice cream shop did indeed exist, and if it did, what flavors of ice cream and toppings it had).

The path curved sharply to the left, and then briefly veered away from the dense trees and out onto an overhang that revealed a breathtaking view of the sea and the rooftops of the village houses below. A few rocky steps led down to a large landing where a big brass telescope offered a close-up view of the scenery.

"Oh, Pax, a telescope! An *enormous* one. I bet it's as big as me. We could easily see the *Mersades* from here. C'mon!"

Pax shot out an arm to stop her. "Jayni! We just resisted an ice cream shop and now you're gonna fall for a telescope?"

Jayni's face fell and she grunted in frustration. "At least

we couldn't *see* the ice cream! *Agh!*"

And so it continued for the better part of two hours—the children alternately helping each other resist multiple temptations to veer off the path, including a ropes course, a six-story treehouse, a picnic blanket spread with all their favorite foods, and a sign that read:

ABANDONED PUPPIES.
ADORABLE.
ADOPT ONE TODAY!

Jayni almost cracked over that one.

"Puppies, Pax! *Homeless puppies!*"

But Pax remained strong—so up, up, and up they kept going, till the sun slid down its western slide and the air turned bitter cold. There was just enough light left to walk maybe another half-mile, and then they would have to stop for the night. Their feet were sore, they shivered uncontrollably, and they were hungry again but out of food. Pax's fears returned, and Jayni griped about the prospect of sleeping overnight on the hard dirt path. The children's breath puffed out in little white clouds, and then something stung Jayni's nose.

She looked up and gasped, "Oh, no. Seriously?"

For floating down from the sky above them were two . . .

six . . . twenty . . . a hundred snowflakes. They fell faster and faster till there were thousands and then millions of them, and the sky and ground quickly turned white.

And now Jayni suddenly knew what the tiny, quilted blanket in her satchel had been meant for. Just like Pax's black cloth, that blanket would have grown to cover them and keep them warm. Shame washed over Jayni again as she realized what a valuable item she had lost because of her foolishness.

Feeling desperate to make up for her mistake, she began looking for cover—a massive tree branch to duck under or maybe some loose branches on the ground with which to make a light shelter. Instead, she spied something much more wonderful tucked between the trees to her right: a small cabin with a smoking chimney.

"Pax!" she shook his arm and pointed. He saw it too and his eyes lit up.

And now the children faced their greatest temptation yet.

"But what about staying on the path no matter what?" Pax asked.

"Declan couldn't have meant stay on the path in a *snowstorm*, right? I mean, we could die!"

"I don't know. I mean, nothing looks better than that warm cabin right now, but what if it's another trap?"

"I know," Jayni said, crossing her arms over her chest and rubbing her shoulders to warm them. "I have a weird feeling about it too, but we can't stay out here and freeze! Do we really have a choice?"

Both stood at the edge of the path, as if the mere sight of the cabin might warm and comfort them. But it only made them more miserable. Pax felt the cold penetrating his bones.

Jayni saw Pax shivering and felt anger well up inside her. "I don't care what Declan said! If he really cared, he would have told us to make sure we were safe, to stay on the path only if it was *safe*! We're *not* gonna freeze to death out here! C'mon!"

And with that, Jayni stepped off the path and into the woods, reaching back to take Pax's hand.

Pax let out a weary sigh as he took her hand and stepped up beside her.

The forest floor was thick with snow-covered, waist-high undergrowth, and towering red cedars stood shoulder to shoulder all around. Just as the children began forging a path through, they were stopped dead in their tracks by a shadowy figure appearing out of the snowy brush. Jayni stifled a scream. Looming before them was a huge animal with blazing orange eyes.

could talk, like every other creature they'd met here, but he just stood there staring them down with those burning eyes.

Jayni's heart pounded, and she lowered her gaze to avoid being turned into a pillar of stone like the evil lord.

Finally, the great cat lowered his body and snarled, "Climb on."

The children hesitated for only a split second, then hurried to obey—even though they were still unsure whether they were being stalked or saved.

They were also unsure of how to ride a snow leopard. There were, of course, no reins, no saddle, nothing to hold on to but the animal himself. But his fur was thick and warm, and the children buried their hands into it and held on tight.

The animal turned around, face set toward the mountain's summit, and as he did, Jayni looked at the cabin one more time. There in the window, staring out at her, was a hideous ghoulish face. She shuddered. They'd almost walked straight into another Bumfuzzle trap. She felt blood drain from her face as she thought about what could have happened had they not been stopped by the snow leopard.

He IS rescuing us, Jayni decided.

The strong, sleek cat sprang forward into the

darkness—dodging trees, leaping over boulders, with steps so silent and smooth that it felt as if they were treading clouds.

It was still snowing, but here under the canopy of tree branches, the children felt only an occasional spray of ice in their faces. The ride was cold but thrilling, and Pax caught himself smiling despite his exhaustion. Jayni thought about the story Declan had told her, wondering if the snow leopard would answer all her questions and explain to her things that even Declan didn't know.

But not right now. The snow leopard hadn't slowed his pace for a good half hour. On and on he raced till the air grew thin and it was harder to breathe.

Pax's ears felt plugged—like that time he flew in a plane—and he knew they had to be near the top of the mountain.

The snow leopard's flying run slowed to a walk. After a minute, he came to a stop and lay down on the ground. The children scrambled off his back, their feet sinking into six inches of freshly fallen snow. They could see no farther than the end of their noses in the dark of this forest, so they grabbed each other's hands and blindly waited to see what would happen next.

Nothing happened.

It was silent and cold. The children stood shivering, waiting for a word from the snow leopard—but when none came, they began to worry.

"Hello?" whispered Pax. "Are you there, Mr. Snow Leopard?"

There was no answer.

"Hello?" echoed Jayni.

The warmth of the snow leopard had protected them from the cold, but now they were exposed to freezing temperatures again, with no way to warm up.

Through chattering teeth, Jayni said morosely, "He's gone. I think maybe this is our punishment for leaving the path. What are we going to do?"

Just then, both children heard a loud *whoosh* and a *flap-flap-flap*. But before they could even guess what the sound was, or where it was coming from, they were snatched up by the backs of their shirts and whisked up into the sky.

Jayni screamed. Pax was shocked silent. It was sheer terror to be flying faster and higher than they'd ever been before—twenty, thirty, then a hundred feet in the air. Two hundred, three hundred feet . . . up and up they went. They writhed and twisted, trying to see what had hold of them, trying to wriggle free—then realizing with horror that if they *did* wriggle free, they would fall to their death.

And fall they did: whatever had hold of them suddenly let go—and down, down they fell, till they crash-landed onto something rigid and scratchy.

Pax looked up and caught sight of the largest red-tailed hawk he'd ever seen. Hawks were a familiar sight on the mountain where he and Jayni lived, but this one was ten times their size. As it hovered on an air current above him, even in the dark Pax could make out its gigantic talons, hooked bill, and a wingspan the length of a school bus.

As Pax stared at the bird, Jayni looked frantically about them, trying to figure out where they were. It appeared as if they'd been dropped into a giant's dirty cereal bowl, but it didn't take long to figure out that it was an oversized bird's nest made of twigs, sticks, pine needles, and bark. Five or six feathers, bigger than Jayni, were scattered about.

The hawk now made a sudden dive downward, sending a gale force wind around the nest. The children were blown off balance and awkwardly tumbled into each other.

Pax righted himself and brushed a few pine needles off his shirt. He turned to Jayni, who half-yelled her discovery: "Pax! We're in a bird's nest! It must be the biggest bird ever! Look at these feathers!"

"I know! Didn't you see the bird above us! It was *enormous*!"

Both momentarily fell silent, still shivering from the frigid air and the fear coursing through their veins. Neither knew what to say or do next. Their predicament was obvious: they were trapped at the top of the tallest tree in the world (or at least that's what it felt like to them), with no way to get down.

Without a word, Jayni carefully crawled toward one of the giant feathers and dragged it into the center of the nest. She did the same with a second feather.

Pax caught on, took off his satchel (which had been slung across his chest the whole time), and grabbed two more feathers, arranging them a few feet away from Jayni's. There were two feathers left.

"We can use those as blankets," Jayni said.

Pax nodded. The two children scooted themselves onto their featherbeds, then reached for their feather blankets and covered themselves. The feathers smelled musty and sweet, like dust and peaches. They were warm and comforting. Jayni lay on her stomach and propped herself up on her elbows. Pax lay on his back, staring up into the dark, starry sky. He laughed a tired laugh. "I guess we're getting pretty good at doing scary stuff, huh?"

Jayni laughed too. "Yeah. But I keep wondering how we're ever gonna get home. Or *if* we're ever gonna get home."

"I know." Pax paused thoughtfully. "I bet I've missed a bunch of appointments and treatments."

Jayni couldn't see it, but there was a faint smile of relief on his face.

Then he quietly said, "Every night before one of my treatments or surgeries, Mom tells me a story. It helps a lot. We could do that right now. Tell each other stories."

"Yes! What kind of stories, though?" asked Jayni.

"Oh, anything. Sometimes it's a story from when Mom was a kid, or a story from a book, or a story she makes up as she tells it."

Jayni pushed herself up onto her knees. "Can I go first? I know *exactly* what story I wanna tell you."

"Sure, Spitfire. Go ahead."

Then Jayni rolled over onto her back, pulled her feather blanket up to her chin, and began, "Last summer when you were in the hospital, I was bored out of my mind, so I read a *lot* of books. My favorite one was called *Gambit and the Old Grey Moon*. It's about this fairy-tale creature named Gambit, who's a chevrotain—that's an animal that looks like a mix between a deer and a mouse—"

"I *know* what a chevrotain is, Jayni," interrupted Pax with an edge of frustration in his voice. "We *both* went to science camp."

"That's right. Anyway, the chevrotain—Gambit—falls through a hole in the ground and ..." Jayni was off and running, retelling the story so vividly that Pax felt as if he were in the pages of a book, not in the nest of a gigantic bird.

The children swapped stories for half an hour, till their words felt as heavy as their eyelids, and their lips could barely get out, "... innn the ... wallls of ... the aaattic ..." Finally, their racing hearts had slowed, their busy brains had quieted, and exhaustion took over. They were fast asleep.

Pax woke hours later, as the black sky lightened into a beautiful sapphire blue. More snow had fallen during the night, covering the nest in a blanket of white. He stayed bundled in his feather bed, not wanting to leave its comforting warmth. The sun began peeking its head between the tree branches. Then Jayni stirred, sat bolt upright, and looked around.

Her face went pale.

"P-Pax?"

"Yeah?"

"This is a *lot* scarier in the daylight."

Pax nodded. Being able to see the sky's expanse above them and hundreds of treetops all around them was nerve-wracking.

"Could you peek over the edge of the nest, Pax? Now that it's light, maybe we'll see a big magical slide or an enchanted elevator or something." As Jayni said this, she pulled her knees into her chest and wrapped her arms around them. She squeezed her eyes shut and took a deep breath.

Pax slowly pulled himself up and out of his bed, coughing, stretching, and rubbing his bald head sleepily. Sometimes Jayni could be so dramatic, but he did enjoy playing the role of protective brother.

"Do you see anything, Pax?"

"Hold on." Pax carefully crawled to the edge of the nest and looked over. "Whoa!" He grabbed tightly to a branch in the nest. "I'm not afraid of heights, but I feel super dizzy. We're *really far up*. I can't even see the ground, and there's not a single tree branch we can reach. It literally feels like we're dangling in midair."

"Pax, what are we going to do? Ugh! We shouldn't have left the path! Why do I keep messing everything up? Why did we follow Wilmer down the Climbing Tree in the first place? And get on that ship? And why did I fall for the Bumfuzzles' trap and convince you to step off the path and—"

"Jayni, look!"

Jayni peered over her knees at Pax. He was pointing to

the thick branch in the wall of the nest that he'd grabbed hold of.

Neither had noticed it in the dark, but a bright ray of sun had suddenly illuminated words carved into the wood. They read:

in the shadow of the wings

"In the shadow of the wings? What does *that* mean?" Jayni asked.

On a hunch, Pax crawled back to his feather bed and lifted one of the feathers over his head like a hang glider.

"The shadow," he muttered under his breath. He looked up at the feather, then down at the nest. "The shadow of the wings," he muttered again.

Silvery tendrils began spinning downward from the feather, like the curly little parts of a grapevine. They twined around Pax and attached to his arms and legs and torso. Then his body began to float upward. It felt as if he were tied to a parachute going up instead of down, with his hands and feet dangling free.

Jayni had wasted no time in grabbing one of the feathers for herself and lifting it above her head as Pax had. Soon she too was securely entwined in its silvery tendrils and was floating upward with Pax.

The feathers lifted them over the edge of the nest and floated between treetops. The sky had exploded into a sunrise palette of pinks and purples and yellows and blues. It felt as if they were parasailing through an artist's watercolor painting.

This time dangling hundreds of feet in the air, Jayni didn't scream, and Pax didn't panic. Both children felt strangely calm and hopeful. Somehow, they knew they were being rescued—by two giant feathers. They left the thick forest of trees and floated out over a precipice that fell sharply into a deep rocky gorge. Then the feathers sailed back into the forest and slowly descended into a clearing between the trees until the children's shoes gently touched down onto the snow-covered ground.

Instantly, the tendrils vanished, as did the feathers.

"Whoa," said Jayni. "They disappeared!"

But Pax wasn't listening. He had caught sight of something out of the corner of his eye and whipped his head to the right. He saw a man, thick and strong, with soft white hair that was speckled gray, a face that was sharp like an arrow, and catlike eyes of yellow-gold. He wore a royal uniform, bleached white, with gold tassels, gold buttons, and red trimmings.

Pax felt his heart leap, and with all the courage he could

muster from his frail body, he stammered, "Are you . . . Sir, are you the—"

But before he could get the words out, Jayni cried, "Lord Zade!"

She stepped forward, but then suddenly remembered she was in the presence of a lord. Not sure if she should bow or curtsy, Jayni dropped to her knees.

Pax watched in bewilderment, unsure of who "Lord Zade" was and how Jayni knew him. He had thought the man was the snow leopard in human form.

"Don't bow to me," the man quickly said, offering Jayni a hand and pulling her to her feet. "I am indeed Zade, but I am a lesser lord. I am to take you to the Great Lord."

"I thought—" Pax hesitated, not wanting to embarrass himself, but also not willing to give up his idea entirely. "I thought you were the snow leopard we met last night."

Jayni turned to Pax in shock. Without hearing Declan's story, how could Pax have even thought of that? Sometimes she forgot how smart he was because of how sick he'd become.

Lord Zade smiled. "I am indeed."

The children gaped at him with wide eyes.

Then Jayni's eyes clouded over. "I'm sorry we left the path last night, Lord Zade. It's just—it feels like there's something evil after us, and then the snowstorm came, and well, I thought we might die!"

"I know it was scary, children. The journey up the mountain always is. But you *have* to trust those who have gone before you. They know the dangers well, and they know the surest way to get safely to the top." He smiled gently. "I was waiting for you in a warm tent with hot food just twenty feet farther up the path."

Jayni hung her head in sadness. Pax wrapped his arms around himself more tightly—partly from the cold, partly from a deep sense of failure. Both of their stomachs growled at the thought of the meal they had missed. If only they had done as Declan had instructed.

"And you are correct," continued Zade. "There *is* an evil after you. It is a grotesque spirit-animal who takes on many forms and employs many hideous creatures to do his bidding. Few have ever seen him in his true form, but they say he is a nightmarish monster. He hates everything good, everything hopeful—especially this mountain. So, from the moment you set foot on the *Mersades*, he has wanted nothing more than to destroy your chances of getting here."

Jayni's mind was racing as she opened her mouth to ask another question, but Pax coughed a deep, wracking cough and winced with pain. Jayni could tell he was suffering. She pleaded, "Please, Lord Zade, won't you take us to the healing man? Could we meet the Great Lord later? My friend is really, *really* sick."

Zade leaned close, his face beaming. "The healing man *is* the Great Lord."

Pax's jaw dropped. Jayni's eyes bulged. The story was true! This enchanted being was just as Declan had described him—a good lord who pointed the way to a greater lord. And the greater lord *was* the healer! Jayni's body tingled from head to toe.

"Come, children. I'll take you to him."

16

The Healing Man

On the path lay a thin layer of crunchy snow, but Pax felt like he was slogging through a river of mud as he followed Zade. Every step was heavy and exhausting. He coughed, took another painful step, then struggled to catch his breath.

Cough-step-gasp.

Cough-step-gasp.

The summit was close, but this felt like the longest and hardest part of the climb.

The path wound uphill to the right, and around one of the bends there suddenly appeared a hunched figure on the ground. Jayni jumped. Pax's heart raced.

For the man was dressed in filthy, threadbare rags; one leg was missing, the other was mangled and bloodied. His arms were covered in open sores, and his bones almost jutted out of his skin.

As they neared, he raised his hooded head, and a face—scarred and bruised, misshapen and deathly pale—looked up at the children. He may have been the ugliest man they had ever seen. Jayni shivered and looked away, but Pax noticed his eyes. They were unlike everything else about him—remarkable eyes, strong like Zade's, beautiful like Darya's, kind like Declan's. These eyes didn't belong in such a terrible face.

The man coughed. A deep, rattling cough exactly like Pax's. And when their eyes met, a large tear spilled down the man's mangled cheek and dropped onto his grimy shirt.

Pax, who understood suffering, could not bear the sight of this man's agony. It was too awful. What had happened to him? He looked to Zade for an explanation.

But Zade said nothing. Instead, with his hands he signaled to the man, and the man feebly signaled back with his one good hand.

Pax recognized it as something like sign language. So, this battered man must also be *deaf*? Was there no end to his suffering? Pax longed to know what was being said between these two.

After a few more signs, Zade smiled at the man, then

resumed walking uphill. Jayni—who had looked away and pretended the man wasn't even there, quickly followed at Zade's heels.

Pax stood his ground, horrified at their hard-heartedness. He knew what it was like to be deathly sick and have healthy people walk right by without a care.

"We need to help this man!" he shouted up at Zade.

Zade turned and looked curiously at Pax. "I thought you wanted to meet the healing man?"

"Of course, I do! But we can take this man with us. He needs healing even more than I do! Can't you see? Look at his—"

But when Pax turned to point at the man, the man was gone. Pax spun around to look down the path, but there was no hint of the raggedy figure. He had vanished.

For the past two years Pax had put on his brave face and silently pushed through endless aches and pains, all the ups and downs, the hope and despair. But this was one blow too many. He slumped to the ground, put his face in his hands, and began to weep. He wept and wept and wept till his body trembled and his eyes swelled shut and his face went numb. He lay there in a heap, wondering if sadness might just kill him before cancer did.

He must have fainted or fallen asleep because the next thing he knew, someone was patting his head and prodding his shoulder and a piping voice was saying, "Wake up! Wake up! You are here! See? Look! Look!"

Pax struggled to open his eyes, still puffy from weeping. His body felt like a lump of lead—it seemed impossible to move any part of it. He lay there, motionless, in that state between waking and sleeping. But those tiny fingers were nudging him harder now, and the squeaky voice almost shrieked,

"Wake up! Wake up! It's—"

"Give him time, Otis," came a deep voice. "Can't you see how tired he is?" The voice had thunder in it, and laughter, and a little bit of music.

Pax thought he must be dreaming, but even so, he forced his swollen eyes open. He was lying on his side, on something like a soft bench, and the first thing he noticed was the floor beneath him. It was made of marbled glass, and underneath it flowed boiling white-hot lava. The effect was shocking enough to rouse Pax from his daze. *Where was he?!* With great effort, he slowly propped himself up onto his right elbow and began taking in the stunning sights around him.

He was in the most magnificent place he'd ever seen—in person or in pictures. It was as if someone had hung a garden upside-down in the middle of the air: above him were grapevines and cascading orchids. All around him grew giant hibiscus flowers (big enough to sit in), fruit trees of every kind (the air smelled like a fruit salad), peonies, and dahlias. Birds sang in tree branches (he could almost understand what they were singing), and something like a cross between a butterfly and dragonfly flitted between the flowers. It was a garden bursting with colors Pax didn't recognize—and even the colors he *did* recognize were so much more brilliant and alive that he wasn't sure they went by the same names: it's as if he'd never seen color before this moment. The wonder of it all took his breath away.

Pax sat up, wide-eyed, scanning his surroundings, turning his head till he almost jumped out of his skin. Behind him stood a little elf, green from head to toe, with small pointy ears, and a face that reminded Pax of a puppy. He wore a pair of denim overalls, no shoes, and a white scarf around his neck. He smiled as if it were Christmas morning—his eyes big saucers of excitement, his hands clasped together at his chin. Pax could tell the elf was trying to contain himself, but finally he squeaked, "You woke up! You woke up! Yay! He's waiting for you!"

And now Pax saw the greatest wonder of all. A man— or was he a giant? A superhero? Pax gaped in awe as the mesmerizing figure walked from behind the elf and around the bench toward Pax.

He was at least nine feet tall and muscular, with dark olive skin, blazing eyes, and white hair that fell to his shoulders. He wore a lightning-white tunic with a gold belt and a glittering sword at his side.

Pax's mouth went dry, his hands clammy. The fantastical being looked down at Pax—who instinctively closed his eyes and braced himself.

"Don't be frightened," he said, in that voice that sounded like musical laughing thunder. "You are welcome here."

And then suddenly, somehow, Pax knew without a doubt that *this* was the Great Lord. *This* was the healing man. He opened his eyes but lowered his head.

"Do you know who I am?" asked the man.

"You're . . . you're the . . . healing man," stammered Pax. He tried looking up into the man's face, but it was too dazzling, too intense. He quickly looked back down.

"Why are you here?"

"I . . . I . . . want to be healed," said Pax. "But"—he added courageously—"I also just really wanted to meet you."

Still looking down, he caught sight of the man's feet. They were glowing, as if a fire burned beneath the skin.

"We've already met once before," the man said simply.

Pax wanted to say, "No, we haven't. I'd remember meeting *you*." But he knew better than to argue with this great man.

The healing man took a seat in one of the hibiscus chairs. By some miracle, it held him up—all nine feet of his muscular body. He leaned forward, resting his elbows on his knees, and smiled at Pax. Pax looked up in time to see the man's glittering tunic, belt, and sword fade into plain clothes, his hair turn a forgettable shade of dark brown, and the brilliance of his face soften. He was still tallish, but besides that, he was now an average-looking man.

Except for his eyes. They were remarkable. Pax wondered where he had seen them before. Strong and beautiful and kind. Pax felt like another world existed in those eyes.

"You've had quite the journey getting here, Pax," the man continued gently.

"You know my name?"

"I do," said the man with a huge smile. "There is much to explain—but later. First, you must go wash and get changed and rest awhile. Otis will take you to your room. Then you will join me for dinner."

"My room? Otis?"

The little elf had begun jumping up and down. "That's me! That's me!"

Pax smiled at him, then looked back at the man. "Where *am* I?"

"In the great palace carved into the mountain—the mountain you just summited. Come."

Head spinning, Pax got up and cautiously set his feet on the glass-marble floor, surprised that it wasn't hot from the bubbling white lava underneath. He stood and followed the healing man, who led him between trees and around bushes of flowers and under low-hanging vines. Sometimes the garden opened into a sunny courtyard or wound around an imposing water fountain. They walked the length of a football field before they came to a balcony at the edge of a precipice at the end of the garden.

Pax gasped. The glass floor disappeared under the balcony and the bubbling white lava spilled out and over and down the mountainside into deep blue water a hundred feet below. Unlike the waterfall he'd seen at the bottom of the Climbing Tree, this was a calm, gentle flow of water, quiet like a garden fountain, even though it was massive and powerful. The lava-like waterfall wasn't the only thing below him. Slightly smaller balconies and beautifully manicured gardens and stone staircases covered the whole of the mountainside. Multiple waterfalls flowed in between and around the landscape, and all the way down to the sea.

"This feels like a dream . . . but it feels really *real* too," Pax whispered, half afraid he would break whatever spell he was under. He continued to stare wide-eyed for another minute, then turned and asked the healing man, "Where is Jayni?"

The man smiled.

"Jayni is here. Otis will take you to see her and help you get settled into your room, which is right next to hers. Now—no more questions till dinner," he said with a twinkle in his eyes.

Otis took this as his cue, grabbed Pax's hand and squeaked in a singsong voice, "Off we go! Off we go!"

"Thank you, Otis," said the healing man.

"Happy to! Happy to!" said the little green elf.

Then the man turned to leave—and vanished.

17

The Dazzling Ones

Otis pulled Pax along the balcony to the top of a staircase that wound down the mountain. Then he dropped Pax's hand and piped, "Follow me! Follow me!"

The staircase was made of ancient stones that looked like they were sewn together with thick green moss. It ran like a curled ribbon down the mountainside, sometimes ducking behind the waterfall, sometimes curving away from it.

Otis led Pax thirty steps down, then stepped off the stairway onto a little stone bridge that led to a little flower-lined path that led to a charming little stone house—a cozy home for one little person. Maybe Declan had stayed here when he met the healing man. A sign hung on the door:

What appears to be
is not.
And what has not yet appeared
will be.

Pax was curious about its meaning, but there was no time to stop and ponder. Otis opened the door without knocking, and Pax ducked his head to follow Otis inside.

The house was anything but little.

In the first room, a dozen people and creatures played instruments and sang—making music so beautiful that Pax wanted to cry and laugh all at once.

But Otis was moving quickly through the room, which opened up into another room where holographic planets and stars floated about in midair. Two animals peered into a large telescope, talking spiritedly about a trip they'd just taken—

"Was it really only a half-million light years away? Why, Ru and Cada were well over *two* million! Let's take those measurements again . . ."

The green elf led Pax into a third room, then a fourth— and the maze of rooms continued, each one leading into the next, each room filled with people and creatures, lively activities, and fantastical décor.

As they entered the nineteenth room, which was lined

with floor-to-ceiling bookshelves, the elf stopped and gestured to a petite, black-haired girl sleeping on an over-stuffed cream-colored couch.

"Jayni!" Pax cried happily.

Before he could reach her, another girl nearly collided with him, as if she hadn't even seen him.

Pax stumbled backward and swallowed a startled cry.

The girl was beautiful and carried a tall stack of papers in her arms—*and she looked exactly like Jayni.* But this Jayni was dressed in a long green gown and was dazzling—and seemingly ageless. She clearly was not ten years old, nor was she any younger or older. This Jayni walked to a table just out of arm's reach of Pax where she joined five friends. Pax looked at the sleeping Jayni to his right, then to the dazzling Jayni on his left.

"It's all here!" she said, setting her stack of papers on the table. "He told me every detail of the story, and it might be my favorite one yet."

Jayni flipped through the stack, and Pax saw little pictures-in-motion jump off the pages. The five friends sitting at the table cheered and clapped, then began talking excitedly.

Pax looked again from the dazzling Jayni to the sleeping Jayni and began to panic. What was going on? Were they cloning people here? Which one was the real Jayni?

But the elf interrupted his reverie by chirruping, "Hurry! Hurry! Your room is next."

Pax was irritated. He wanted answers, not more questions. But when he remembered he'd be able to ask the healing man his questions at dinner, he resigned himself to follow the elf into the next room. And what he saw there gave him the shock of his life.

The room was a science lab—or maybe a hospital operating room. Pax couldn't decide which.

A man peering through a microscope shouted, "Look what I've found, Doctor! Come quickly!"

Another man's head popped up from behind a desk piled high with books and technical instruments, and Pax almost fainted. It was he, *himself*—a second Pax, but ageless and dazzling like the second Jayni. This Pax had a full head of hair, his arms were strong, and his face glowed. He walked over to the man at the microscope, stooped over, and peered into the eyepiece. After a few seconds, he stood up and clapped his hands.

"Barton, you did it! You found it!" exclaimed the second Pax, slapping his friend on the back. "This is exactly how he described it to us. Catalina, come see. It's marvelous!"

A young woman took her turn at the microscope. She whooped and hollered alongside the two men.

Pax trembled. He looked down at the elf. "What's going on? Why is he exactly like me?"

"That's not a question for Otis!" the little green creature squealed. "You'll have to ask the Great Lord!"

Otis skipped over to the room's balcony and pointed to an overstuffed hibiscus chair with a view of the sea.

"Rest here! Rest here! Fresh air is good! I'll come back soon!"

He waited till Pax had sat down, patted Pax's arm with his tiny green hand, then turned and romped out of the room.

18

The Weeping Boxes

Pax tried to rest but he couldn't. Seeing a healthy, thriving version of himself kept his heart and mind racing till Otis returned with Jayni—his *friend* Jayni, not the other one. Finally reunited, the two friends talked rapidly, almost breathlessly, as they walked behind Otis who led them out of the house.

"You met him too?"

"Did you see what we looked like back there?"

"What does it all mean?"

And so they chattered away as the elf took them through a grove of tulip trees till they came to an open door in an ivy-covered wall. The children followed Otis through the doorway into a vast garden that made their runaway conversation come to a screeching halt. They gasped.

Extending the length of the seemingly endless garden sat a seemingly endless table surrounded by thousands of feasters and overflowing with food and drink: fresh loaves of bread, clusters of grapes, grilled meats, goblets of sparkling apple cider, hunks of cheese, towering cakes, colorful salads, berries and melons of every kind, chocolate fondue, and oversized mugs steaming with . . . popple-cream! Glasses clinked, flatware tinged, and the feasters chatted away as they ate with gusto. The conversation was lively, happy, and punctuated with laughter—and no one argued or interrupted or appeared to be left out.

Otis led the children to two empty seats—directly across from the healing man.

"Dear children!" said the healing man with a smile that made his face glow warm as an ember. "Sit down and make yourselves comfortable." He reached for a carafe of sparkling apple cider, then poured two goblets full and set them in front of Pax and Jayni.

"Fill your plates! Fill your plates!" squeaked little Otis before he spun around on his heels and skipped away.

Now that they were seated right next to the others, the children were shocked to see how dull and lifeless they appeared in comparison to everyone else. The others were radiant, strong, blazing with life and color. By contrast,

Pax and Jayni felt weak and wispy, like morning fog.

Pax tried to muffle his cough and hide his weakness, for he was well aware that no one else here was sick or disabled or in pain. He felt so out of place—and yet, with all his heart, he wanted to belong here, with these people, with this man.

Jayni squealed as she heaped her plate high with food. Pax slowly followed her lead. He was hungry, but even more so, he was overwhelmed with the thoughts and emotions pulsing through him. Distractedly, he placed food on his plate, blindly stuck his fork into it, and lifted it to his mouth.

The healing man looked at him with those eyes that seemed to know everything.

"So. You want to be healed."

Pax's eyes lit up as he took his first mouthful of food. It was by far the most delicious thing he had ever tasted (in fact, he was convinced he'd never tasted food until now), but he hurriedly swallowed and choked out, "Yes, sir. I want to be healed more than anything."

"And what will you do if you are healed?" asked the man.

The question surprised Pax.

"Well, I'd go back to school full-time," he said thoughtfully. "And I'd play soccer again. And I wouldn't be bald anymore. I'd eat without getting sick. I'd stop coughing all the time, and I wouldn't be . . . afraid of . . ."

"Dying?" The healing man's voice was full of compassion as he finished Pax's sentence.

Pax's eyes filled with tears before he could stop them.

"You have suffered so much, Pax," he added quietly.

Those six little words did something inside of Pax—like a key unlocking a room long shut up.

Jayni sniffled beside him and said in a voice husky with emotion, "He has, sir. He's suffered *so* much."

"And so have you," said the healing man, locking eyes with Jayni. "It is no small thing to care for a sick loved one."

The three fell silent as tears streamed down their faces and they exchanged knowing smiles. Pax was amazed that the healing man was crying with them. After a few moments, Jayni finally ventured a question she'd been wanting to ask for some time.

"Sir, what should we call you?"

The man smiled as he answered, "You can drop the 'sir.' Just August."

Jayni pronounced his name slowly, with both awe and adoration, "August. I like that name."

"And now I can see by the look in your eyes that you have many more questions for me," said August. "But before I answer them, I have something to show you. Come."

August rose from the table, and Pax and Jayni eagerly got up and followed him. They walked back to the ivy-covered wall, and the children noticed that the wall had not just one door—the one through which they'd entered with Otis. It was lined with doors as far as the eye could see. Round doors, tall doors, ornate doors, every kind of door imaginable was half-hidden under the thick growth of ivy. August explained that each one led to a different country of the world or corner of the universe.

Jayni had to keep herself from shrieking with delight and flinging them all wide open. The journey to get to the healing man had been humbling and hard, and Jayni had begun to wonder if she were losing her sense of adventure. But here in this place, with her best friend and August, she felt her courage and joy returning. She almost bounced as she walked in between August and Pax along the enchanted wall.

After passing twenty or so doors, August stopped in front of a clear glass door and pushed it open. He walked forward a few paces, into a brightly lit glass room, then stepped up onto—thin air? The children raised their eyebrows and looked at each other. August proceeded up an invisible stairway, and, curious, the children followed. Sure enough, there were solid steps beneath their feet as they ascended behind August, but all they could see was the glass floor retreating beneath them. The invisible staircase led them up and out into a marsh, where they walked over moss-covered stones, then across a pond by way of lily pads. Jayni giggled and said she felt like she was walking on water. Pax tried bouncing on the lily pads and was surprised at how springy they were.

Finally, after ascending a gentle bluff covered in lush green grass, they came to a building made entirely of jewels—diamonds and emeralds, rubies and opals. It glittered and shone in the sun. Like a city skyscraper, the towering structure boasted two massive solid-gold doors, which August opened wide for the children.

Inside these doors was a vast palace of treasure chests—millions of them, stacked from floor to ceiling in all shapes and sizes, as high and as wide as the eye could see. Like the building, these were also made of precious stones and jewels. Some were the size of a tissue box; others were the size of a bedroom. But it wasn't just the beautiful boxes that captured their attention. The children also heard voices—weeping, wailing voices that seemed to be coming from inside the boxes themselves.

Startled and confused, they both looked up at August.

"This is one of my favorite places," he said.

"But the voices!" declared Pax. "They're awful. Where are they coming from?"

August explained, "These boxes hold great treasure—so great that all the wealth in all the history of the world could not compare to what the smallest box here contains."

He continued. "But the treasure was bought with suffering. It was through great pain that the owner of each box acquired their wealth. And although they no longer suffer, their tears still cry out—to remind us how costly and precious their treasure is."

"You mean, people hurt so bad, it made them—*rich*?" asked Jayni.

"They hurt with hearts full of hope and courage," said August. "They suffered believing that one day everything would turn out for good."

"Did it?" asked Jayni, still not fully understanding.

August nodded his head.

Pax had been listening with one ear to August, but another ear to a voice that wept louder than all the others, and now he turned to follow its sound. He walked past row after row of glittering, weeping treasure chests, till he came to a box so big and beautiful, he froze in his tracks. It was tall—so tall he couldn't see the top of it. The wailing coming from this box was almost unbearable. Pax wanted to cover his ears and run away, yet his curiosity compelled him to stay.

August and Jayni caught up to him, and all three of them stood there, staring and silent.

Finally, with a trembling voice, Pax asked, "What kind of . . . Whose box is . . . " His voice broke. He'd believed no one else could understand his suffering. But on this journey, he kept coming face-to-face with others' pain and grief.

August walked up to the enormous treasure chest and gently ran his hand over the front of it. "This one is mine," he said.

The children's jaws dropped open as they looked at the healing man.

"*Yours?*" asked Pax.

"Yes."

"But how? What happened?" asked Jayni.

August didn't answer. Instead, he slid his hand across the face of the box, revealing a window to the inside. The children eagerly stepped forward and peered in. At first, they could see nothing but darkness, but August said,

"Keep looking." At the same time, they spied a pile of dirty, bloodied rags in a heap at the bottom of the box.

Pax looked over at August. "It was you! The man on the side of the path! *It was you!* That's why . . ." Pax's throat choked with emotion and tears sprung into his eyes. "That's why you . . . understand."

Jayni was slowly beginning to put the pieces together herself, but it was difficult to believe that the rag man could also be the healing man.

The children both stared at August. Something inside them was waking up, stirring, growing. This healing man understood every kind of suffering—Pax's, Jayni's, Declan's, all the citizens of Dree, every owner of every weeping box.

"You're seeing into the Everworld realm, children," said August with warmth in his eyes. "And the longer you look and listen, the more you will see and understand." Then he added, "There's something else I want to show you."

He motioned for them to follow him. August walked past a dozen more rows of treasure chests, turned left, took a few more steps, then stopped and pointed to two boxes. One was made of onyx and trimmed in topaz. On the front was the word PEACE. The other was made of diamonds and rubies, and it read, FAVOR. Both boxes constantly changed size—one moment they could fit in the palm of your hand; the next moment, they were big enough to hold an elephant.

"Pax. Did you know that your name means 'peace'?" asked August. His voice was soft and tender as he added, "This is your treasure box."

Pax didn't blink. He just stared at the box, listening to its wailing.

August turned to Jayni. "And this is yours, dear one. Your name means 'favor.'"

Jayni was quiet for a moment as she took it all in. In a hushed voice, she finally asked, "Why do they keep changing sizes?"

"Because you still have more life to live and many more choices to make. These boxes may be quite small when you finally come to live here—or enormously large."

Jayni dropped her gaze and asked quietly, "Will I get a small box since I haven't had cancer?"

"Oh, child, life in your shadow world is hard, even without cancer. Suffering comes in many forms. But joy comes when you understand that *this* is the real world, here with me, and all those troubles in your world won't last forever."

"*Shadow* world?" asked Jayni.

"Yes," said August. "Your world is fading fast, like a shadow—as are you both. That's why you seem almost transparent here in this realm. But soon you will be free of all shadows, all pain and sadness, evil and grief—and you will grow strong enough to experience the Everworld in its full power."

Pax finally found his breath and asked, "Sir . . . I mean, August—was that *us* back in those rooms? You know—the other Jayni, the other Pax? Are they us in the future?"

August smiled. "Yes. Since time works differently here —no clocks or yesterdays or tomorrows—in reality, you both are here already."

"Whoa!" exclaimed Pax.

"That's amaaazing!" said Jayni.

"We looked like *superheroes* back there!" Pax added.

"Then"—Jayni paused, as if summoning up the courage to ask—"then Pax gets healed?"

"Yes," said August carefully, although Jayni thought she saw a hint of pain in his eyes. "Pax *will* be healed, but it will not come in the way you expect."

As Jayni opened her mouth to ask what he meant, August laid his hand on her shoulder and said, "It is not for you to know when or how."

A heavy silence followed. Jayni looked sideways at Pax,

who was taking another long look around him. Then he turned to August. "I think maybe I'm starting to understand. I'm okay with not being healed right now." Pax paused and took a deep breath. "I'm glad that no matter what, things turn out good in the end."

"Better than you can imagine," said August with a huge smile that made his eyes gleam again. "Come—let me show you both more of what you have to look forward to!"

With that, August grabbed their hands and led them through more mysterious rooms and gardens. He let Jayni open one of the Doors to the Universe. (She had a hard time choosing between Paris and the moon Titan, but Paris won in the end.) Pax explored the Enchanted Entryway that served as a sort of invisible curtain between the Shadow World and Everworld. It stretched as a rainbowlike arch across a small meadow bordered by magnolia trees. When he looked at the iridescent arch from the side, it disappeared entirely; but, if he walked directly up to it and stuck a hand through it, his hand disappeared.

August introduced the children to people who they felt they'd known all their lives. They laughed and played and worked and explored with August till their hearts were bursting with more happiness than they'd ever thought possible.

The children pelted August with questions all along the way, most of which he answered. But to a handful of them he said with a smile, "That is not for you to know yet."

The Return to Shadows

The sun did not seem to rise or set, no one slept as there was no night, and the children could not feel any time passing. Meals were eaten only occasionally (but what magnificent meals they were!). The longer Pax and Jayni were there, the more wonderful it was. They dreaded when it would come to an end. But they knew it would have to.

It was just as they were pondering whether they'd been in the Everworld for a year or just a second (for it felt like both) that they heard August say, "I have one more thing to show you before you go."

He transformed back into his fantastical form. His plain clothes were replaced by the lightning-white tunic, gold belt, and glittering sword. His eyes sparked into flames, his hair shone, and his feet glowed. He took their hands in his, and they were catapulted into a kaleidoscope of stardust and sunbeams. Misty air whipped at their faces, their feet dangled free beneath them, and then suddenly they were standing at the top of the mountain path that had first led them to August.

The children blinked in surprise. How dull everything here looked now! The sights and sounds and smells seemed almost drab in comparison to what they had just experienced. Even August's shining appearance turned plain once again. Their faces fell.

"It *is* a shadow world," moaned Jayni. "I'd never noticed it before."

"Yeah, it looks kinda *see-through*," added Pax.

"It's hard to come back, isn't it?" August asked tenderly. "I'll be plain with you, children: it doesn't get easier from here. There's more suffering ahead. But in the end, it will seem like only a pinch of pain. In the blink of an eye, the bright and beautiful parts of the Everworld will overtake the shadowy parts. And then you'll be back with me— for good."

"Oh, August, I can hardly wait!" cried Jayni.

Pax sighed heavily. "It doesn't *feel* like it will come quickly. I don't want to go back. Please, August. I want to stay with you."

"That's how you *should* feel, Pax," said August. "That desire will help you on the hardest days. But it's not time yet. You have a special job waiting for you back home. You too, Jayni."

"What is it?" asked Jayni eagerly.

August held out his hands to reveal two little boxes— exact replicas of Pax and Jayni's treasure chests, marked "Peace" and "Favor." But these boxes didn't change sizes or weep. He placed them in their hands.

"These boxes will remind you of me. The Everworld has filled you with strong joy and hope, but the shadows of your world can make you forget what you've experienced here. Put these where you can easily see them— and remember me often. Then help others see what you've seen."

"Just like Declan did," said Pax quietly, finally understanding.

"Yes, like Declan," said August, his eyes gleaming. "You would never have made it here if he hadn't shown you the way. Now it's your turn to do that for others who are hurting."

"How?" asked Jayni. "Do we take them through the tree? Like Wilmer did? Or, how else do we get them here?"

"When the time comes, you'll know what to do,"

answered August. "Now, follow the path back down the mountain, and rejoin your friends."

He said this in a tone that meant there would be no more questions and no more answers.

Without a moment's hesitation, both children threw themselves into August's arms. He hugged them tightly and then looked down at them with his stunning eyes— those beautiful, strong, kind eyes that said "I love you" without saying it at all.

And then he was gone.

Pax and Jayni stood motionless, staring into the empty space August left behind. They looked at each other and began to laugh, and then to cry—and as they held on tightly to their treasure boxes, Jayni said, "We should go, huh?"

"Yeah. Let's go home, Spitfire."

Down the mountain they hiked, still stopping now and then to let Pax catch his breath or rest when the pain grew too great. But the pain didn't seem to matter as much now. There was a reason for it, and there was treasure waiting for him at the end of it.

They walked courageously past the monster's cabin, the treehouse and the rope swing, the ice cream sign, and the dead dragon snake. It all seemed much less impressive now compared with August and his Everworld.

They talked excitedly about every detail of their adventure, reliving every marvelous moment. They struggled to find words strong enough to describe what they'd experienced, so they ended up saying "amazing" and "unbelievable" over and over again.

As they reached the bottom of the mountain, they saw that same little wooden sign with the strange words—the ones they'd not been able to read before:

In mundo patiens—Spero!

All at once, both children could read it clearly and they said aloud together,

"In a suffering world—Hope!"

Then they looked toward the sea, and Darya was rushing toward them from the beach; Wilmer was flying at breakneck speed (or "break-knee speed" as he would say); and Declan brought up the rear, hobbling as fast as he could. His face was beaming, for he could see their faces, and he knew they'd been with the healing man.

The sun was sinking low when Pax and Jayni found themselves standing beside the Climbing Tree's trunk.

What time was it?

What day was it?

Had it all been just a dream?

They looked at each other with eyes full of wonder and questions.

"Do you think—" Pax began, but something glittering on the ground caught Jayni's eye.

She grabbed Pax's arm. "Look!"

There at their feet lay two jeweled boxes, and beside the boxes were several tattered brown feathers. They bent down to pick up them up.

Pax, holding a feather in one hand and the box marked Peace in his other hand, whispered, "Then it *is* real."

Jayni nodded, tracing the word Favor with the tip of her finger. "It's real."

They scanned the area around them, half expecting to see a beautiful nymph or a bumbling bird or a little peg-legged man come bursting through the trunk of the Climbing Tree. But everything was as it always had been.

The sharp scent of pine filled the air and a cough tickled Pax's lungs as he breathed it in. "I bet they can see us," he said.

"Definitely," agreed Jayni.

Then, with their treasure boxes in hand, the two stepped out from underneath the tree's heavy pine curtain. The sky was pink, the birds chirped their evening song. The children took a few steps in the direction of home, then Jayni linked her arm with Pax's and sighed happily.

"I'm glad we followed Wilmer into the tree."

"Me too, Spitfire. Me too."

POPPLE-CREAM RECIPE

While in Everworld, Pax and Jayni heard the story of popple-cream. The drink was originally created for seasick sailors hundreds of years ago, but somewhere along the way, the recipe was lost. After years of searching for the recipe, explorer Perry T. Piffle discovered the brittle remains of a parchment labeled "popple-cream" inside a bottle and hidden in the deep recesses of a sunken ship hundreds of miles south of Dree. All the ingredients listed on the parchment are legible except one, and while many experts have attempted to decipher the smudged word, no one conclusively knows what the mystery ingredient is. We strongly recommend you add whatever secret ingredient you wish. (Perhaps a dash of cinnamon? Or a drop of melted white chocolate?)

Research shows that popple-cream tastes best when enjoyed with friends or family.

Popple-cream

1 can full-fat coconut milk

1 cup unsweetened almond milk (or oat milk)

3 tablespoons unsweetened cocoa powder

3/4 teaspoon monk fruit extract
   (or a small spoonful of honey)

3/4 teaspoon vanilla extract

1/4 teaspoon almond extract

Pinch of sea salt

Mix all ingredients together in a saucepan. Heat on the stovetop on low, whisking constantly, about 3-5 minutes. Do not let popple-cream boil. (That will just bumfuzzle everything.) Pour into mugs. Serves two adventurous children or one chilly Hobblechaun.

To read a special letter from the author,
visit colleenchao.com/ShadowWorld.

ACKNOWLEDGMENTS

Amanda Cleary Eastep: You breathed life into every page of this story. Had I searched the world over, I could not have found a better editor than you. Thank you for the gift of your unparalleled editing skills, your loving wisdom—and your dear friendship as we labored together. This book would not exist without you.

Catherine Parks and Trillia Newbell: You were the first to say, "We want to see this story published!" And then you went to work to make it happen. Your faith and encouragement mean more to me than I can put into words.

The rest of my Moody team—Connor Sterchi, Melissa Zaldivar, Erik Peterson, Avrie Roberts, and so many others: You are the best publishing team a girl could ask for. Thank you for your vision to publish children's fiction—and for letting me be a small part of it. I love working with you all.

Benjamin Schipper: Thank you for your artistic prowess that has given even more meaning to my characters.

Reece Book: You know this story inside-out—and

although I've wept over your suffering, I marvel at God's hand in your life and the stunning beauty He's creating in you. Thank you for giving me insight into Pax.

Ethan Langley: You will always be my "super-port buddy"—and one of the inspirations for this story. I'm so grateful the Healing Man has healed you sooner rather than later.

Dr. Haghighat, Paige, and my entire dream team of clinicians and staff at St. Luke's Cancer Institute: I worked on this book while you took such beautiful care of me this past year. Thank you for letting me bring my little workplace into yours—and for gifting me so much joy and laughter as we worked alongside one another.

Eva, Noah S., Ghilly, Micah, Aaron, Kylie, Noah K., Kaci, Brooklyn, Katelyn: You were my first readers four years ago, and your insights and excitement gave me courage to share this story with a larger audience.

My nephews and nieces: Aaron, Kylie, Ethan, Caleb, Daniel, Elise, Joshua, Ellie, Christopher, and Esther: I wrote this with the prayer that you will be Declans and Daryas in your world. You each bring me more joy than you can possibly imagine.

My parents and siblings (Pops and Mommers, David and Heather, Jonathan and Shawna, Jeff and Kates,

Christopher, Nathan, Daryl and Marie, Justin and Amanda): Your encouragement, support, prayers, doorstep drop-offs, long-distance visits, convos over good food, laughter, and love have strengthened me for this writing journey. I'm so glad you're my people.

My five besties: Nina Buser, Karen McCutcheon, Lisa Hamel, Carlynne Alberts, Wendi Kuhl: You cheered and prayed this story from its inception to its binding, never once doubting that God was in it all. I feel the gift of your friendship on every page—and could not have written this without you. (And Wen, I'm still gaping at how God wove your own story into this one—long before we knew.) I adore you girls.

Eddie and Jeremy: You are the reason I write—and the reason I fight for more time here. I'm so grateful these shadows don't last forever, and we have an Everworld of joy waiting for us. I love you fiercely and forever.

And to my Jesus: Your love has filled my heart to overflowing. Your presence has beautified these shadows. Your voice has whispered purpose into every pain. You are my Healing Man, and I adore you.

Is it possible to face the darkest days of life with hope and joy and purpose?

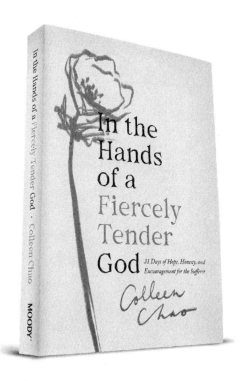